MW01118591

The GrandDad Tree
A Novella

By
Thomas Dobbins

Cover Art
Jason L. Petersen

Cover Design
Dave Dobbins

Anna —

Enjoy your read!

Tom Dobbins

Bailey Woods **Publishing**   *Redbrush*

God's peace Always —

Bailey Woods Publishing

ISBN: 978-1-7355231-0-1 (Printed Book)
       978-1-7355231-1-8 (E-book)

For
My Shelly

NIV (Philippians 2: 5-11)

"In your relationships with one another, have the same mindset as Christ Jesus: Who, being in very nature God, did not consider equality with God something to be used to his own advantage; rather, he made himself nothing by taking the very nature of a servant, being made in human likeness. And being found in appearance as a man, he humbled himself by becoming obedient to death— even death on a cross! Therefore God exalted him to the highest place and gave him the name that is above every name, that at the name of Jesus every knee should bow, in heaven and on earth and under the earth, and every tongue acknowledge that Jesus Christ is Lord, to the glory of God the Father."

Early morning routine: open the shade on the front door to let in some early summer warmth. Crunch on some cereal and milk while checking the newspaper headlines. Finally, the coffee's ready so I take my cup and paper and settle on the front porch to breathe in the day. Birds going crazy to greet the sun. If you don't mind I'll brag on my coffee. It's so good, just as it was yesterday. In fact, my coffee was great all last week and the week before and all month long. I drink it black. It's just that good.

I love this part of the day, and the coffee is so good I have another cup before I have to leave for work. I'm on the early morning shift because the other folks don't like being early every day. So I have to get on my way quick and open up at 6:30.

That was my routine. It didn't change a whole lot from week to week, month to month. Not thrilled about being the only one at the shop at 6:30, but that's my job. I've been at the print shop for nearly 5 years. I guess that puts me at 23-and-1/2 years old. I feel older than that. But I walk to work quickly, like a young man in good shape.

It feels so good walking or cycling in the early morning quiet, especially since I quit smoking. That's not entirely true. I just had a cigarette with my second cup of coffee. So, after that first smoke of the day, I might have only one or two more during the day. Yeah, I've cut way, way back on the smoking habit, and now even pedaling my old 10-speed feels easier.

Morning routine at the print shop: unlock everything, turn on all the lights, get the small utility press warmed up and ready to run. Check the bathroom to make sure it's clean enough. Turn on the coffee maker (the coffee is lousy at the shop). Quickly check the front office for any orders that came in late yesterday, so I can start setting up for the first press run of the day. Check the phone messages. Check the chemicals in the darkroom.

My brother! He told me the day before about this oddball dream he had. (Damn it.) Nothing was going to mess with my morning ritual of getting ready and opening up the office to get everything lined up for the day. Just a dopey dream but, yeah, I guess you could say he was interfering with my routine.

I did some re-touching of the negatives that we processed the day before. I checked all the presses and loaded them with paper so they could run most of the morning. I dumped the recycle bins. I hauled three heavy bags of trash out to the dumpster in the alley. Marie arrived with a box of donuts at 7:15, said "hi" and got busy with her accounts at her roll-top desk.

CHAPTER 1

Colt's Dream

My brother (he's only 12) told me all about his dream:

He said it started with walking through a small room. It was dark, but he could see light ahead in the next room so he kept walking. There was an open passage into the larger room which looked like a library. He saw nothing but books. There were bookshelves on all the walls loaded with all shapes and sizes and colors of books. The only other thing in there was a ladder. It was one of those rolling ladders you can slide around in order to reach the high shelves. So he started climbing the ladder.

He looked at books as he climbed up. They seemed to be organized or grouped into sections, like a public library. He kept climbing, but the ladder continued with no end in sight. And he climbed and climbed with nothing else to see. Books were everywhere. The more he climbed, the more the ladder began to shimmy. It didn't feel as safe, but he kept going as if he needed a particular book.

He clung to the ladder as it wavered and rolled a little side to side on its wheels down below. Shelf after tall shelf was crammed with books. Then there was something different, so he climbed a few more steps to see what it was. In between books on a shelf just out of reach was a blue rubber ball, about the size of a kids' soccer ball. He leaned over and reached for it. The ladder quaked and rolled under him so he gave up on the ball and continued.

Then something happened: the ball moved. He saw it out of the corner of his eye, starting to roll. He tried to slide back as the ball moved on its shelf. He reached down for it. The blue ball rolled over the edge and fell. The ball disappeared, but he could hear it bouncing, bouncing and echoing from the floor below. So he climbed all the way back down the ladder, but he couldn't find the ball anywhere.

Why a blue ball?

"Daron, can you help with a customer, please?" Marie was calling from the front counter, and I was up to my elbows with cleaning fluid. I did the best I could with wiping down the print rollers, then wiped the dark crud off of my hands with the dirty rag. Next to me John-the-Printer was in the middle of a press run on the small offset. He just shrugged.

The woman waiting near the front door looked familiar, but I couldn't think of her name. "This is Mrs. Fleury," Marie said. Maybe everyone in our little town knew this gentlelady, but I recognized her only as the one who lived in the huge old house. It was a grand mansion, and it was just over the bridge at the east edge of town. "Can I help you?" I said, hoping my hands weren't completely gross from cleaning solution.

"It's just a small printing order." She handed me some pages. It was something from the Bible—that I could tell right away. "It's from the book of Romans. Chapter Four."

I looked at Mrs. Fleury with her shiny, loopy earrings and silvery-bluish hair touching, almost, the collar of her suede jacket. She seemed to know who I was. She was asking for some kind of reproduction of a chapter from Romans, and my thought was, "Is this public domain?" Probably. So there shouldn't be any hassle about it.

"You want a chapter re-printed?"

"Yes. But what I want is just one page. Just one verse from Chapter Four. That's all I really need."

My baffled face must have had that look that I tend to have when someone throws me a curveball. Maybe I just stared back at her or we stared at each other. "Can you help me with this?" Mrs. Fleury asked with her polite smile.

"Uh. Yeah. I mean, I think so," I said, weakly trying to return the smile. Was this the oddest request ever? "Uh yeah, sure, how many copies do you need?" I wrote "Fleury" at the top of the order form and tried to think of something else to write.

"Just one."

I looked up. "Just one … copy?" Over my shoulder, I could tell that Marie was enjoying the scene.

"Yes. Just one. Just one page, actually."

I made that sound with my mouth and lips when you shoot out some air that you've been holding in your lungs. Maybe they heard me, maybe not. I didn't mean anything. It just sort of oozed out of my mouth. Why is the boss never around when these things happen? I scribbled something. I didn't know what to ask. It seemed like she needed a Bible chapter, but she was only interested in one part or one line or one verse or —? From Romans. Chapter Four.

"So," I babbled, "we'll do a job for you, and it's a reprint of Romans and you only need one chapter, but you just want a single verse?"

"Something like that. But just do it any way you like as long as I get Chapter Four. And Verse 18. Just one page is all I need." I could tell she was trying to help me with this puzzle that had landed in my lap. "Make the job easy for you. You'll be helping me a lot," she said. "It's my favorite verse. It really focuses my faith."

"Sure," I said. What else could I say? This gave new meaning to our company phrase, "full service printing." I turned back toward the shop and told her, "We'll get started on this. Check back in a couple of days, and we should have something for you." Marie was still chuckling.

Later, I tried to explain the one-page, one-verse job to John-the-Printer. You should have seen the expression on his face.

CHAPTER 2

These days when I get home from work at mid-afternoon, it's nice to relax on my front step and watch the folks passing by. The apartment is just a block from Main Street so the noise isn't bad. This is my time to pick up my book and a cigarette (my second one that day) and finish off the coffee I made that morning. I'm about half-way through "Zen and the Art of Motorcycle Maintenance." But I was interrupted by my little brother, riding over on his bike. He likes to hang out with me after school sometimes. He had a big plastic cup of soda with a straw.

"Having a smoke?"

"Having a Dr. Pepper?" I replied, sounding just a little snarky. "And yeah, I just had my second smoke of the day, all right?"

Colt, with his goofy glasses held on by a strap at the back, plopped down on the step and slurped soda through the straw. The glasses made him slightly bug-eyed. He can be a pain in the ass, sure, but I suppose I am, too. I'm kind of glad he's comfortable riding over to my place so he can get away from Mom for a while. She's kind of depressed and quiet these days. Very quiet.

It was funny, I suppose, when Mom and Dad decided to have their third kid, and along came Colton in 1970. Funny, because I was born 11 years earlier and didn't want a new brother or sister. I guess we eventually found our groove with three kids all spread out. Rachael was kind of stuck in the middle. Our sister didn't seem to act like either of our parents. She was just Rachael. Now, she was somewhere in the hinterlands with her high school boyfriend. Mom has been not quite herself ever since Rache disappeared.

Colt has enough weird ideas to make me roll my eyes at least once a day. He does this weird thing where he flips his hair around. We sat there a while feeling the sun roast our skin, and he said, "You know that dream, the one I told you about?"

"Yeah?"

"So? You've been thinking about it?" he said.

I wasn't really looking at him, and I put my feet up on the railing. Maybe the trees were more interesting. "No, not really. You want me to? I'm kind of busy these days." A blue jay landed on the railing and peered skeptically at my coffee mug. "Everybody has kooky dreams, right, kiddo?"

Colt wobbled his feet in some kind of rhythm and watched his floppy shoelaces. Something was rattling around in his little head, but I just waited for it to spill out. We both waited, and I reached over and shuffled my hand through his out-of-control curls of dark brown hair. The early-summer sun was already softening his mop to a lighter shade.

He snorted a little and spat over into the grass. "Hey, Daron, guess what?"

"What, Bro?"

"That dream, climbing that ladder and all those books…" He paused. "It's not a dream."

I looked at him. "Huh?"

He nodded. "Right. Not a dream. It's real." His eyes were shiny but dark.

Sometimes Colt reminded me more of Dad than anyone. Dad could be goofy or do something bizarre, totally out of the blue, although he was a hard worker and serious guy, mainly. We were just your typical small-town family unit, right?

I suppose. But then —around four years back our Dad died, so…

"Guess what, Colt? You're nuts. No, really, I mean it. Why do you keep yacking about that dream?"

"Listen!" he said. "I've been wanting to tell you. I knew you wouldn't believe it … Listen! I'm not making it up. It's real. I really saw that place!"

"You saw a place?" I said with a snort. "Where? You went to this library, and there was a ladder? A ladder on wheels? What is wrong with you, man?"

"Daron, listen! I can't tell Mom or anybody. Only you. You don't believe it but I can show you. I'll show you it's not a dream!"

I just don't know about this squirt of a brother. What am I going to do about him?

"I'm busy, Colt. You're not going to show me anything."

The Dream, continued:

Colt turned back through the dark room into the "library" with its shadows and light. He looked around at the familiar scene. Was there a particular book he needed? There was no blue ball in sight. He went to the ladder and climbed.

It was scary, that wobbly ladder, but somehow it had to be "safe" because it had to be connected up above. He gripped the sides to keep his balance, so there would be less wavering. He looked at books and titles all the way up. Some were geography books and atlases and maps, but nothing really special.

He saw that he was already higher than the first time. When it felt like the ladder was shifting, he would grab the solid wood frame of the shelf until he felt steady, before climbing on. He also found that the ladder would glide easily to the right or to the left so he felt more in control. But when he looked down, it was as if the hard, tiled floor was a mile below.

Geography, maps, history, psychology and more and more collections … nothing that grabbed his attention. And a little higher up he noticed some law books, architecture and a religion section. He stopped climbing.

There was something just out of reach. He moved the ladder slightly so he could see better. He tried to reach over and grab it, but it was too far. He pulled the ladder again to the right, and again he failed. Was it a sheet of paper? Or maybe several white sheets, poking out between two books. His fingers tried to grasp for it. If it was just a blank sheet, why would he need it? Once more he gently shifted the ladder an inch or so, but then it wouldn't budge. He couldn't touch the paper. Reaching, he felt the strain in his shoulder and back. It was an inch or two away, sticking out from the books. The ladder was stuck.

Giving up, he felt he might as well start back down again. It was smooth going, and he wasn't scared about the ladder any more. He was about halfway down when it happened, and it took his breath away.

The whole structure of the "tower" of books above him began to move. He blinked, and his eyes tried to take in the sight of the slow collapse of the tower. He quickened his steps down the rungs but kept focusing upward, feeling vertigo as the internal view moved down, and every book was in motion —slow motion. His foot slipped and he grabbed the ladder, clinging for dear life. Upper sections were pulling toward him, but the pull was inside-out. Or, was it outside-in? Books, shelves, even the top of the ladder—all in motion —down, down. His entire field of vision filled with motion which somehow pointed at the top of his head. His eyes couldn't take the visual any more so he blinked and quickly looked down. There wasn't a sound besides the shaking of the ladder under his feet.

Glancing back up, he saw that the scene was changing again. Books and shelves still moved, but now the direction changed. It began like a right-angle turn. Just over his head, or maybe at an arm's length, it gradually shifted away and to his left. What had been inside-out now swung horizontal. Motion now pushed away from him. It was more of a stretching view as it turned. The ladder also bent to the horizontal. Everything that had been above was now pulling away from his left shoulder, and the motion slowed. And came to a stop. He clung to the ladder with every ounce of strength his muscles could give.

Just trying to breathe, he stepped down the vertical portion of the ladder. Every step was deliberate, and he kept his eyes ahead. Descending the last portion felt much slower, but at least there was progress. Step followed step, down and down, and finally—he touched bottom. Leaning against the ladder, he felt a wave of relief. He had to get out of there. Just as he turned away he stole a glance back up. The solid tower of shelves, books and ladder was just as vertical as before, straight to the vanishing point.

That's what he told me—and it was almost as if he described something real.

CHAPTER 3

The boss makes it in to our little shop when he feels like it, which isn't that often. I don't think he knows the difference between a four-color offset and a paper cutter. He seems to know nearly nothing about operations and darkrooms, but at least he knows how to go out and sell a print job. And maybe he does all right with re-supplying our paper and ink. I just wish he'd manage to be here when there's a customer like Mrs. Fleury. He's a big man and takes up a lot of space. He's noisy. He wants you to know he's there so he sort of rumbles around, talking out loud but not making much sense. That's how he feels important, I guess.

When he leaves, the place is quiet and we can get some work done. The next day, John-the-Printer and I figured out how we would reproduce the Romans 4:18 single sheet or chapter. We would have her take a look at a proof and see if that's what she had in mind. I think the boss was downtown at the Rotary Club or something.

Later on, Colt was supposed to come over and eat dinner with me. I rode my bike back to the apartment to be sure I had it all under control before he rode over. With not a lot of food in the place I figured I could offer either macaroni and cheese or something with sausage. It occurred to me that I might even combine the two. No doubt, Colt would really enjoy the dining experience.

He threw down his backpack and bike at the front step and looked around the kitchen before even saying "hi." What he did say was, surprisingly, "I'm hungry."

"Yeah." I said. "Food's ready. How's Mom?"

"She's okay. She worked at Kroger's today." He was wearing his Alice Cooper t-shirt. "She says you never come over any more." Yeah, well, I thought, maybe I've been busy.

"It hasn't been that long. Tell her I'll come on over soon. Has she heard from Rachael?"

"Nope." Colt looked at the plate I handed him. "What's this?"

"It's mac-and-cheese. With sausage."

"Looks like crap." He tasted the mac-and-cheese, from Kroger's. "What's this meat?"

"I told you, it's sausage. Turkey sausage."

"What's turkey sausage?" He poked at it with his fork.

"It's sausage," I said, "made from turkey." He made that face to show how utterly untrustworthy I was. Then he ate everything on his plate in about two minutes. He was up and scrounging the cupboard for a box of cookies while I started on my meal.

"Glad you could come over, Colt. I thought you might be hanging out with that friend. What's-his-name." All I could think of was something like "Flipper," but I didn't want to guess.

"His name is Bilder," said Colt. "But we started calling him Blink."

Right …"Blink." So much easier than Bilder. I didn't think my brother had a lot of friends. Blink was the one with hair a shocking shade of yellow. "So, he's your best friend, right?"

"I mostly hang out with Blink and Gregg. We call him Grill."

I was pretty sure Gregg was the African-American kid. He was smaller than Colt but built like a little lumberjack. "So, what have you and Gregg and Blink been doing lately? Riding your bikes?"

"Sometimes we ride our skateboards at the park. What else is there to do?" He took the last chocolate chip cookie from the box and crammed it in his mouth.

"Right. I used to do that. Which park, the new one?"

"No," he answered, "the old one. With the old stone bridge." Oh yeah, the "old" park, the one where I used to hang out.

"Colt, remember you and your friends need to be careful around there. Not always the best people in that park."

"I know," he said. "They put all kinds of graffiti on the bridge and everywhere. But, we're careful and we don't go at night."

"Good." I watched as he tilted the box for the last few cookie crumbs, then finally gave up on finding anything else worth eating. I was reaching for my half-cup of leftover morning coffee when he brought it up again.

"Daron, I need you to go over there with me, to the park."

"Yeah? How come?"

"There's something I've got to show you. Please come with me? We can go now, okay?"

"No, we're not going to the park. You've probably got homework, and Mom will be wondering about you."

"You've gotta come with me! Please. I can't show anybody else. If we go now we'll be home way before dark."

I stared him down as only a big brother can. "Hold on —this isn't anything about that goofy dream, is it?"

"Listen, you're my Bro, right?" he said.

"Don't argue—"

"Just come with me. And I won't even say anything about your non-existent girlfriend." Nice. My brat of a brother. How do I kill him and get away with it? "Colt—"

He was already on his way, like Rocky the Flying Squirrel out the door and yelling as he grabbed his bike and backpack: "Meet me over there, okay?"

By the time I reached the porch he was out of sight.

Colton was waiting at the park on top of the old stone foot-bridge. That viewpoint was a meeting place for my friends and me back when it was still a functional bridge with a storm culvert running beneath. But years ago they re-graded with a slope and sod on the north side of the bridge to divert the runoff. Now that it was blocked you could only go partway under the south side.

I was still catching my breath from jogging over to the park when I saw him looking down from the stone arch. "What the heck are we doing here, Colt?" I was sputtering. "You got something to say? It better be good after you drag me all the way over here."

He scurried down below and started poking around underneath. The artists, with their words both profane and banal, had painted every surface. He was pushing on one of them, a kind of slab that fit the original opening under the bridge. I hollered, "Don't be messing under there!"

"Come here and I'll show you," he said. Now I could see that someone had tagged the surface with scrawling red letters: "Mo SLAME!!" That's where Colt pushed against the slab, and it started to move. "What the—?" Maybe the upright slab didn't actually move like I thought. But then he gave it another little shove, and on the third push it definitely moved. The slab swung away and up to reveal a dark opening.

"Wait—" I said, but he was on his way through. "COLT!" I scrambled underneath and peered into darkness. He was nowhere in sight. "Colt!" The kid could really haul when he wanted to, but didn't I have to catch up? I pushed into the cave which was the one thing I absolutely didn't want to do. Where was he? There was some kind of an underground room, small and shadowy. I headed through shadows to a light on the other side which turned out to be—

A library!

My eyes couldn't take in the sight. Impossible. This wasn't real—it could only be a kid's wild imagination. Light…books…shelves…a ladder…my brother, standing on the other side. My feet couldn't move, and my mouth hung open. This had to be some kind of dream—but I was in it. Suddenly he ran behind me, and before I could even squeak he was in the dark area and closing the slab. "NO!" was all I could manage.

"Don't worry," he said, "I checked it. We can always open it back up."

Nothing made sense. I could only whisper: "Colt—what … what is this place?"

"I don't know, a library?" I looked at my brother, I looked at the books, and I looked back at my brother. We were surrounded by ancient, deeply stained mahogany or pine. Shelves, supports and ladder beckoned with their silken surfaces. We were somewhere under the earth near the old stone bridge, and there was a ladder reaching up—where?

Colt pointed up, and my eyes followed his view. I couldn't see the top of the ladder. There was a vanishing point far, far above our heads. My brain was a hollow place. "Who—Why—?" My whisper echoed somewhere nearby. He was at the bottom of the ladder, stepping onto the first rung. I shivered. "How did you find this place, Colt?"

"We were at the bridge, Gregg and I, just messing around. I came back later."

"But … you knew there was a door—?"

"It was loose. I could tell by pushing," he said. "But I waited until Grill was gone." At the ladder, I was still craning my neck to see where it all went. Did it actually reach several stories high? "What are we doing here?" I said.

"Will you climb it for me? I need you to find something up there." My heart was still pounding, and my breath was a gasp. I looked up the endless ladder he wanted me to climb. "What's up there?" I tried to swallow. "We need to get out of here."

"Daron, will you try to get it for me? It's a piece of paper. I think it's just past the architecture section."

Architecture? Section?

"Listen, bud, we don't even know how this place can be here. This—this can't be … What's up there that's so important?"

"It's not that far, really," he said. "I was up there. You can reach it for me. Please?" My head throbbed a beat in time with my racing heart. Colt was asking me to find something that didn't exist, inside a place that didn't exist. Except in my addled brain. "Bro, really, is this a dream?" As he moved aside I stepped onto the bottom rung of the ladder which felt solid, and my hands shook. I looked back at him. I took that first step and then another.

"I'll hold the ladder steady for you, D." It was good, I suppose, that he was below as I began. It felt steady, but where was the ladder connected? And would it roll around under us? But I was on my way … to something. "You're doing good," he said. I gazed as high as possible, but there was no "top."

Climbing the impossible, I looked at books on either side. Edgar Allan Poe and Mark Twain, John Steinbeck and Flannery O'Connor. James Baldwin and Toni Morrison and John Updike. Willa Cather, C. S. Lewis and Shirley Jackson. Then we were past the modern authors section and into Biology and Geology. Anatomy and Astronomy and Agriculture. Then it was Floriculture and European Colonization. Then, oversized maps, atlases and Geography. I climbed slowly and the ladder felt almost secure, and Colt was somewhere down below.

Eastern Mysticism and Pre-History. African Art. Romanticism, Oceanography and Accounting. 20th Century Economics and Cookbooks … followed by World War II. Pest Control and Stonemasonry. Carthusian Spiritual Practice. Lepidopterology.

"Are you keeping me safe down there?" With a quick glance I could tell he was slowly following me but closer to the bottom. "Yeah, don't worry—I'm keeping it stable for you, Bro," he answered. His voice sounded small. I was just passing the Gun Collecting section. I thought maybe we were nearing our goal, but once or twice I asked myself: why in God's name are we here?

"Hey, you said Architecture, right?" I said. "Yeah," he replied, "but go just a little farther past that section."

Then Colt said, "I think I'm going to be an Architecture someday."

"Architect," I corrected.

"Whatever."

After my climb of what felt like half an hour, but was more like a few minutes, I made it past Architecture into what I guessed to be

British Colonial Literature. And there it was, the reason we were on this expedition. I saw a paper poking out from a couple of books. So, maybe this wasn't a dream? Just a few more steps up, and it was in reach. Or was it? I wanted to get that paper and be done with this frightening task. But I couldn't quite touch it. "I can't get it," I hollered.

"Slide the ladder over a little. I'll help you," said Colt. When we grabbed the framing we could pull a few inches. The ladder quivered; my hand was shaking. My fingertips touched it now, but just barely. "A little more?" We both pulled and, finally, I could get two fingers on it. It wouldn't budge. I pulled again and tried not to look down. I felt the slightest movement so I didn't give up. I pulled with finger and thumb. I held my breath. The paper moved, and I pulled. I grabbed a little more, and it moved and started to slide, and I gripped it hard. One more yank and it was in my hand, but my hand was shaking and my arm hurt.

It slipped—

I lurched to my right holding desperately to the ladder with both arm and leg. My last grab—and I caught it! I clung with both hands to keep it from falling. "You got it!" yelled Colt. My whole body trembled with exertion as I hung on to the ladder, praying not to slip. "NOW," I yelled, "Now, let's get the hell out of here!" But I took one moment to look at it. It was a white envelope rather than a single sheet, and it had something written on it. I held the envelope securely and slid it under my belt for the climb down. "Go!"

Colt led the way, and I followed his steps down the ladder. I wanted out of this freakish world under the sod, so I headed down much faster than the upward climb. "Down! Go faster!" He tried to move quicker, but his legs were small and that limited his movement. But we made progress as the various sections and groupings of books slid by.

"Hey, Daron, there's something else I meant to tell you," he said. He was stepping off the bottom, and I was fast approaching. "There's this weird thing that happens with the top, when it twists and slides down."

"What the heck, Colt?" It felt so good to have solid ground under my feet. "Can we just get out of here?"

"Remember the dream? When I was here, everything started moving and twisting over my head and coming down. It didn't fall, but everything sort of turned and went sideways." I had no desire to look back up where he was pointing, and what he said made zero sense. I grabbed my brother and jerked him back toward the blackness of the cave. "Out! Move!"

"I'm glad it didn't collapse on us this time, though," he said, and I shoved him again for good measure. He found the panel in the dark and gave it a little push, and it lifted up as if it were spring-loaded. Outside, where I expected nightfall, we stepped into a sun-bathed park. I was relieved that no one else was nearby. Over my shoulder I took a glance at the undisturbed gentle slope just beyond the bridge. Where was the infinite tower of books?

Colt pushed the Mo SLAME!! panel back into place and then reached toward the envelope under my belt. "Let me see it!" I yanked it out and we both looked at the front side, where something was stamped in the upper left corner, in black.

From the desk of:
Ilsa Manningly

It appeared to be a printed or embossed envelope. It was sealed. I turned it over and saw something written in blue ink, and it looked like a woman's careful handwriting:

"I have a message for you."

Nothing else. Just that sentence on a plain, white square-ish envelope. I turned it over again and looked at my brother. "What is this?"

He shrugged. Checking again to be sure it was sealed, I asked, "Should we open it?"

"Yeah!"

I pulled out my pocket knife. Good idea? Bad? I didn't hesitate long. I sliced the envelope open, and we both looked. Empty—nothing—not even a tiny shred of paper inside. "What the—" I said for about the eighth time that day. Man, did I need a cigarette.

CHAPTER 4

John-the-Printer was at the front counter with Mrs. Fleury. I was finishing up a contact sheet in the darkroom, for a brochure project. When I came out John was showing her the proof for the Romans Chapter 4 verse. The lady with the sparkly eyes and jewelry was saying something about how long she'd waited before doing this. "But I finally decided to have something made in honor of my father-in-law, Raymond. He was such a sweet man." She held up the proof and said it looked just right, and she even said, "Suitable for framing." I kind of stayed back to listen.

"This Romans verse sometimes reminds me of another one," she was saying. "That one about unbelief." John nodded and waited for her explanation as she took a slip of paper from her purse to read. "For me, though, it is about my faith in Jesus Christ … It's from the Gospel of Mark in Chapter 9: *'And straightway the father of the child cried out, and said with tears, Lord, I believe; help thou mine unbelief.'"* (KJV)

John, with his big sloppy printer's apron and grimy fingernails, nodded again and smiled at Mrs. Fleury. He thanked her and said we'd have the final print ready later in the week. She smiled back and said good-bye to John and Marie as she left the shop. I knew John well enough that he was taking this seriously, and the final product would be perfect, even if it was a little weird.

Yesterday I was climbing a ladder, retrieving a secret, and today I was calculating and repositioning for a four-image spread. Last night I tried to sleep but didn't quite manage, thanks to a memory of a billion or so books in stacks a mile high. And I had found an envelope.

Or, did I? I had joined my brother in some kind of fantasy. And there was something else: a new wrinkle. From above my viewpoint on the ladder as I grabbed Mrs. Mannningly's "message," I glanced up and saw something like a top railing. I would need to go back to confirm, but it seemed the ladder might be connected to a higher support or maybe a circular walkway. Which meant another trip below (or above?) the old park to know for sure if there was a walkway going … somewhere? Which also meant I would have to tell Colt, and he would be ready to race back to the park. And, he would want to climb even higher than before. At a place that didn't even exist.

So, it was a relaxing walk home at mid-afternoon. Maybe I could think about some other stuff for a while. The phone was ringing as I walked in. I answered, with a pretty strong suspicion who was calling. "Hi, Mom."

"Daron, have you seen Colton?"

"No."

"Usually he's in and out of the house after school. But I haven't seen him or his bike…" She sounded a bit flustered. I turned toward my front door in case he was just arriving. "Mom, he's not here. I'll go look for him, but I don't think there's any problem. He'll show up."

"He might be with one of his friends," she said, "or—I don't know…"

"I'm on my way." I rode my bike over toward Mom's thinking I might intercept him or run into Gregg or Bilder. I was really hoping that Colt wasn't doing something stupid like re-visiting the "Library" on his own. So I was relieved to see him on his skateboard, heading home.

I hollered: "Hey!" and caught up with him. "You may be in trouble with Mom. But she's not too mad. Anyhow, don't mention the 'Library'. Not to your friends, not to anybody. Okay?"

Colt said, "I haven't said anything about it. I was over at the bridge today, but Grill was hanging around so I left."

"Listen, man," I said. "And I mean this: don't ever go to that place without me. Got it? EVER." He nodded and picked up his board.

"Okay, D, I won't."

We headed to the house, where Mom waited and watched at the door. I was hoping there might be some food. Mom looked tired, and she was wearing some sort of a dark reddish sleeping jacket over her work clothes. I saw her book, something by Bronte I think, opened up next to her recliner. My mom, a tiny woman, had dark brown hair (streaked with gray here and there) that she wore loose past her shoulders. Or, sometimes she'd tie it back. She was telling Colt how he'd messed up. The lines in her face were a contrast with pale, soft skin.

"You know you need to let me know what you're up to, and don't make me wonder about you," she said, or something like that. She didn't sound mad, just concerned that he wasn't checking in. I jumped in: "Yeah. Come on, you're old enough to be responsible. Don't make Mom worry."

"Oh, shut up. What do we have to eat?"

After dinner, which was square fish fillets and carrots with ranch dressing, I was ready to go home to bed. On the way out I had my usual query about Rachael. Mom said, "Nothing new, she called and asked for money."

"Then she told Mom to 'pound sand,'" Colt said. I looked at Mom's eyes, and what I saw seemed a new level of sadness.

Colt followed me out the door. He whispered, "When can we go back there, D?"

"Tomorrow. After work," I said. I gave him a friendly little smack on the top of the head, and he swung his leg out to kick me, but I dodged. I pedaled home in 10 minutes and, after a couple of swallows of cold coffee and a smoke, I was ready to catch up with my book. I nodded off after a while and dropped into a short dream. I was somewhere near the top of a tall, quaking ladder. When I started to slip I looked down and couldn't see anything below. I lurched to one side and reached out for a slippery pole, and then I was starting to slide down. The more I slid the more my feet swung out, and I was spinning like a top, faster and faster, legs flailing, down, down.

———————— ❧ ————————

I drew the short straw, or something, when John-the-Printer was finally satisfied and handed me his one-sheet job for our newest customer. It was a beautiful parchment but only after a number of tweaks and attempts by John for his usual perfection. I drove over to the lady's house in the company car, passing through that archway of ancient trees sheltering a couple of stately blocks along Wellington Ave. As usual Mrs. Fleury was happy to see me and couldn't hide her delight at the "suitable for framing" print of Romans 4:18.

Framing was just what she had in mind, she said, in memory of Raymond. Then she said she was honoring both of her in-laws, who had built and owned the mansion for many years. It was the most beautiful house I'd ever seen with its broad stairway and tall, leaded-glass windows. It gave me the urge to touch things, inspect the window closures, smell the varnished banister and listen for the creaky floorboards. Along the hallway a door or two seemed to lead to secret places—or maybe just a cellar. A detailed painting of a grand peacock dominated a plastered wall of the vaulted dining room.

I started making excuses about getting back to work when she wanted to give the complete tour, so she showed me her picture wall where the new framed print would have a special place. The center of the display was an ornate carving of a Celtic Cross. She pointed out photos of the young and the old, including her late father-in-law and mother-in-law. I peered at their faces, especially the wide-eyed babies in fanciful baptismal gowns.

Mrs. Fleury explained, "When I see these old photographs, especially the children, they stand out as a single moment of time. Do you ever try to capture a moment? That's where we live—I believe—in a precise instant of time. Because that's what God grants to us."

CHAPTER 5

Back at the office it was a day to wrap up odds and ends before jogging home on a sweet late-May afternoon. Unfortunately, though, I first had to lock up when both Marie and John called it an early day, and the boss—well, who knows? Finally, I made it to my place, and Colt was waiting. "Where've you been?" was his greeting.

"At work. Like I told you."

"Can we go now?" He was already reaching for his bike. What's with this kid? Why so anxious to re-visit "the place"?

"Hang on," I said. I wanted to grab the Manningly envelope to take with us. When I took it out of the drawer and looked at the writing on it, it didn't seem real and nothing about the next chapter of this mystery could possibly be real. Yet, the "real" envelope was now safely tucked in my pocket.

Colt rode his bike along the street as I walked and jogged over to the old park. When he tried to wander off I yelled and told him to stay close. "Any time we go back to the park, we're staying together, got it? And, remember, you don't go there on your own, okay?"

"Right," he said. We made it, and he pushed through the little swinging doorway. I made sure that some nearby kids weren't paying attention before I followed Colt inside. It was creepy in the dark entry room, and I wanted to be in The Library. I bumped something with my foot. A blue rubber ball rolled out of the shadows and stopped near the bottom of the ladder.

"Look!" he hollered. "My ball! You found it!" He bounced it on the hard tile floor. "Well…" I said. Why was there a blue ball, just as Colt had said? It had fallen from one of the bookshelves. Whose ball? Colt's ball?

"Okay, don't make so much noise with it. Leave it here on the floor. Come on." I headed for the ladder. For some reason I wanted to climb as fast as possible, so I was maybe a third of the way when I realized that far below my brother was bouncing and bouncing his ball. "COLT!" I yelled. "Get moving! Climb up with me … are you coming, or what?!" But he seemed to be waiting.

"D—" he called up, "I wanted to see if anything would happen, you know, if the top starts to move…"

As if on his command, it started. Somewhere above my head the world was changing. A movement, a turning, a twisting. Slow, slow motion. I shook my head. My neck ached from looking up at the slow twist. Like Colt's old-timey baby toy that spins, the book tower and ladder turned toward me and onto itself. Turning, it then reversed and, slowly, the whole thing moved right at me, and it reversed again. How fast could I get down that ladder? Somehow my feet were on the solid ground in about five seconds. There was a slow burn behind my eyes.

"Look!" He motioned over our heads as I gasped for air. And I saw above that everything was back to absolute normal. But, wasn't it just on the verge of collapse? "See," Colt calmly explained, "it's what I was wondering. It only happens when one person is on the ladder, but if we both climb, we'll be safe."

"Yeah? Well, maybe you could have warned me? Geez!" My heart was still rocking my chest.

He didn't say anything. I reached for the ladder, not really wanting to climb. "So, you're right behind me all the way?" He nodded. Back on the ladder, I stepped up cautiously and slowly, watching all the while for any weird shifting overhead and listening for anything that might break the silence. I could hear his steps right behind me, so that was a little bit of comfort. We climbed through all the familiar sections, including the one where the envelope had been.

I think I noticed some of the Sherlock Holmes stories as I made new progress, then I looked back at Colt and shouted, "What the hell?" He was awkwardly trying to carry the ball under his arm. "No, man! Why would you bring that with you?" He struggled up a few more rungs with the ball while clinging, one-handed, to the ladder. "Drop that!!"

"No, I may need it."

"DROP IT, Colt!"

"No!!"

"You little—!" I let out a sigh which is what older brothers do. With every movement the ladder vibrated a bit, and then I saw him stuffing the ball into the open backpack. (Okay, that was clever.) There was no sign of any strange twirling or shifting above, thank God, and eventually I glimpsed the narrowing "top"—or at least what I thought I'd seen on the previous climb. That goal seemed reachable, and I focused my energy and vision on finding out if there was an upper railing or not. Then we would get out of there.

"Is it getting shiny up there?" I asked.

"Yeah, maybe?" he said. Or maybe it was an illusion, but it seemed there was more light. I hadn't identified any light source so how could it be turning brighter? But I definitely noticed, and we could now see the end of our climb. There was a railing. The "top" was somewhat narrower than the floor level far below us, and the ladder was attached with wheels to the circular walkway. Which made the whole scene even weirder, because our climb had felt almost vertical rather than at a sharp angle.

Impossible: somewhere above that top railing we saw clouds and blue sky.

CHAPTER 6

There are days when you feel everything is approaching perfect beauty. This may not have been that day, but I had never seen a sky that beautiful. Blue like the truest of late October afternoons. The softest of white downy-comforter clouds, all floating in balance like sweetness and harmony and happy days somewhere over our heads. The view was of perfection and completeness. It couldn't have been more inviting if an angel voice said, "Follow me to commune with Mother Nature" or something.

We were almost there with just a few final steps to ascend. Then I was on the walkway, and Colt was just behind me. It was a relief after all that climbing to have something under our feet. The walkway circled around from where the rolling ladder was connected. Then, a couple more steps. I hesitated. Where were we? Was this where we were supposed to be? We could easily be in danger or maybe we'd die up there or couldn't find our way back.

Regardless, we had arrived. Colt and I looked around at the landscape of some kind of shimmering green grass or even some kind of crop that had been planted in rows. It was lush and green but almost artificial. It grew beneath our feet, and that field swept all the way to the horizon. Our eyes took it all in: the growing greenness and the little paths or trails that wandered here and there, inviting our feet to follow. We gazed at the blue and white shining sky which was a layer of peace and hope.

"Are we going to live here?" My brother sure had his way of asking the most weak-brained question that plopped between his ears.

"What do you mean 'are we going to live here?'" I asked.

"I don't know." He was looking up at the clouds. "Maybe we just need to be here or something. For some reason."

Well, sheesh, wasn't it obvious? I didn't say it, but of course we were there for a "reason." A Purpose. A Guiding Principle. Or some other puzzle that had dispatched us to this weird planet where you could choose from three colors: green, blue, white. Somebody or something was behind this whole scheme, right?

"I don't know, either," I said. "Let's just try to figure one or two things out. Like who built this place, you know—I mean is this somebody's idea of a funny joke or is it serious?"

Colt walked ahead of me a few steps. "Looks pretty serious to me." With his backpack slung over one shoulder, he scuffled his feet through the green undergrowth and stepped onto the path. The blades of grass or plants were very springy; they even had a coiled form. But soon enough it was obvious that nothing was actually moving in the wind. Because there was no "wind." The clouds which had appeared to be floating by were actually stationary. There was a feeling of air moving against our skin, but nothing moved. Nothing. Just dead calm.

"Wait," I said. "When we walk we have to find our way back." Over my shoulder was the walkway whose circle crowned the whole structure of the tall "Library." But what if we lost sight of it? I hustled back to that top section and hoisted up two armloads of books. Balancing them on the railing, I made a meter-tall stack with a bright red copy of "The Wizard of Oz" on top and rejoined my brother.

"We'll keep an eye on that stack and the red book on top." Colt nodded and took off toward one of the trails. Following him, I must have checked back for that easy landmark a half-dozen times. So we walked. And walked. Trails wandered off in random directions, and we followed. The surface under our feet was a little springy but something like an artificial composite where lots of people walk—like an airport. Since we had no idea where to go, I simply trailed along as he tried this or that meandering path. I glanced back. There was our marker, our book-stack, always visible. Our anchor.

He was the first to say it: "We're getting nowhere." We had walked for maybe twenty minutes, and the trails led us here, there, and back. The green twirly grasses were everywhere. It was all the same, and the books were behind us, always. Circles, triangles, infinity loops—you name it, we tried it, but good old home base seemed not that far away.

Once, we headed away from each other on twisty trails in opposite directions. In two minutes we were face to face, eyeball to eyeball. Was there a "horizon"? I don't know, because the surface seemed to slope gently downward, but we never found a border. We found nothing. Air touched our skin, and clouds held their positions in that painfully blue sky. We stopped, we started, we stopped again. "Let's go back," I said.

What was the point? Colt then asked, "Did we try that path over there?" Of course we did, and he knew it. "Let's go back," I repeated and with a new sense of anxiety. But nothing changed, and the landmark was there in the distance waiting for our return. We headed back, and Colt started bouncing his ball. "Don't do that," I said. He bounced again. I could hear his steps just behind me, and every few steps he would bounce the blue ball, making a dull, muffled sound. "Knock it off!"

A few more steps and he bounced again. "Colt!" I yelled. He had stopped, now holding the ball, eyes bulging at me through his lenses. I'd never quite seen that look in his eyes. He whispered: "Did you hear that?"

"What?"

He stared. "I heard something. Just now. Didn't you hear it?"

"No. Come on. Keep going."

"Daron, I heard a voice." I froze, hoping to get the hell out of there but not knowing what to do next. "I heard a voice, D. I bounced the ball, and it said something."

"No, you didn't." I glanced around for anything new or different.

"You didn't hear anything, and I didn't hear anything. It's just your ball making a noise, and I told you to stop bouncing."

He bounced the ball twice—and I heard a voice.

"Come on!" I yelled and took off, not even caring if he was running behind me. All that mattered was getting back to the stack of books, and I made it there in less than a minute. But he wasn't behind me. Then I saw him, and he was taking his sweet time, walking, holding the ball. "Colt!" I was getting close to the end of my rope with this kid. He finally approached, and I almost wanted to pop him for being so casual at a time when I wanted to panic. But there was that look in his eyes again, and he said, "Listen." Again, the bounce of the ball and this time there was no doubt. There was a voice.

"Myles," said Colt. "Who is Myles?"

My voice was shaky. "I just want to climb back down," I whispered. "Okay?" I was on the steps and heading for the walkway and ladder.

"It said 'Myles'" he said as he followed. "Do you know anybody with that name?"

"I don't know what I heard," I answered, "but no—it wasn't 'Myles.'" It felt good to be back on the ladder, but still I was looking back over my shoulder.

"You heard something, D. What did you hear when I bounced the ball?" It takes concentration climbing down an endless ladder. I didn't want to think about anything. Yes, I had heard a voice, and maybe it said something like a name. Or, not.

"It sounded like 'while' or 'a while' to me," I said. "Not Myles. Keep climbing."

"A while?" he asked. "So it sounded almost the same for you, didn't it? Maybe a name or maybe it sounded like 'While'? But those words sound almost the same, don't they?"

I was too occupied with my descent to let out a big-brother sigh, so I just said, "Yeah, Colt. They sound similar. We heard something. Let's keep going." Weird, for sure. How in the world could a voice speak to us in the muffled echo of a ball? Somebody's name. Or something else. It was an empty place, even if we had a sense of being watched. Our fantasy world now had a sound. Why? Besides, if a voice wants you to hear something wouldn't it be clear as crystal, not garbled?

"Aren't you glad I brought the ball, Daron?" We were finally close to the bottom of our long downward trek.

"Yeah, bud. I'm glad you brought the ball up there," I said. "And your backpack."

"Do you think Myles has anything to do with Mrs. Manningly?"

This time I did sigh. "Shut up, Colt."

CHAPTER 7

Later in the week, I was on the way back into work after delivering a box of business cards across town when I saw Mrs. Fleury in the office, talking with Marie. They were old friends. That's what I judged from the way they were happily chatting about stuff. After saying hello and making my way back toward the shop, I overheard something about Mrs. Fleury's father-in-law, Raymond, whose photo I'd seen in her home. I hung back a little to catch some of the conversation.

"And, you remember him, don't you?" she was saying. "And at his funeral, there were so many people. A few hundred at least, but it seemed like thousands of friends. He influenced so many."

"Mrs. Fleury?" I said. I had slipped through the door to the front office. "Sorry—I thought I heard you mention your father-in-law? I remember that special dedication you made for him."

She glanced at me, then back at Marie. "For some reason my thoughts go to Abraham whenever I remember Raymond." She chuckled. "Not that he was a great holy prophet or anything, but I guess it has to do with leadership qualities." With that quick flash of a smile, I thought I saw a gleam of silver in one of her teeth. "My husband was a good man, a fine man … maybe I didn't always turn to him with a personal challenge. In our family and especially from a woman's point of view, Emery's dad was the one you would seek. He was the strong leader of the clan, you might say.

"And when I read about Abraham in the Bible, he seems to be such a man of God with a trusting heart and spirit. In my situation, or maybe for anyone—we all need that to lean on. It's almost as if Raymond is still with us as a figurehead. A leader."

I wasn't quite sure what to make of all this, as Marie and Mrs. Fleury wrapped up their talk for the day. But it gave me the idea to look up Abraham when I got home that night and maybe read up on him. About all I understood was that he was some kind of patriarch in the Bible. I thought I might also check with Marie later on, to see if she had anything to add. She was alone in the office when I came back up to the front that afternoon.

"Hey, Marie. I didn't know the lady's father-in-law or her family. Did you?"

Marie appeared to be shifting cards or shuffling stacks of papers on her desk. I knew she had her own system for the accounts, and nobody bothered her about it. But it wasn't anything I could begin to follow. She spoke up over the muted rumble of John-the-Printer's press.

"Well, of course you might say that everybody knew the family, back in the day. But I didn't have a lot of connection with them. Mainly just through the social club that Renda and I and your mother belonged to." Renda? I guessed that was Mrs. Fleury's first name. Marie added, "Are you about to wrap it up back there in the shop? I'd like to be on my way before too long—if you can spare me."

"Sure," I said. "John and I are just finishing up the last run for today. We'll clean up and lock the place for you. Thanks for the info about Mrs. Fleury's family and Raymond and..." I paused. "I guess I don't know her mother-in-law's name."

"You mean Ilsa?" she asked.

Uh. Uh. Uh ... What? What did she just say? "Ilsa?" My tongue got stuck somewhere in my mouth so I couldn't swallow. Or say another word. Or breathe. "Yes," Marie went on, closing down her roll-top desk with a satisfying "k'chunk."

She locked her desk. "You've heard of the Raymond Manningly family, haven't you?"

Ilsa and Raymond Manningly? You might say the next trip back to The Secret Place would take on new significance. We now had a name, and maybe a face, but nothing to clear up the message.

When I got home that evening I spent some "time in the Word," looking up Abraham in the Old Testament. (Also known as "Abram," as I discovered.) So, when God called this sort-of nomad and his wife, Sarai, into holy service, they more or less pulled up everything to follow the command. They were really old but they became parents anyway, and a whole new generation got going ... and going, and going. I learned that a branch of genealogy in the Bible is devoted to the line from Abraham all the way to Jesus. That's a pretty significant connection, you might say. Even King David is in that line from Abram/Abraham.

The deal is, or so I learned—Abraham is this sort of patriarch of the whole Bible who is like the father or grandfather of the Hebrew people. There are all kinds of connections in the New Testament, also. Abraham even had to make a choice whether to sacrifice his own son! Can you imagine?

I might want to ask someone about this. Who was I kidding? The only person to talk to now was Mom, although I was a little—reluctant—to bring up the subject. Mom had a Savior. She'd never really tried to push any of that Jesus stuff on me. (There was that time, though, when she said God is pursuing each and every one of us. I still remember her saying that.)

I knew I could count on her love—and I had a feeling about where that love came from. When I got over there she was reading something by C. S. Lewis. Of course, her Bible was open nearby. I hoped Colt might be out of hearing range, so it was good that he and Gregg were absorbed in one of those squealing video games in Colt's room. Mom didn't seem at all surprised when I brought up the Bible topic in our conversation. With that faraway gaze she listened and then lowered her head for quite a while. It was a long time of thinking, a very quiet time. I wondered if she might not answer at all.

"I'm not the ideal one to answer a question about faith," she said, finally. Deep, dark eyes looked back into mine. "All I can do is ask my own questions. Like—where are we going? You might be surprised that I pray all the time. ALL the time. Lots of questions, waiting for answers. Wondering." There was another long pause, then, "And, yes, sometimes there are answers."

Prayer? This had taken an unexpected turn. All I had in mind was something like what is the Mary-Jesus-David-Abraham connection ... or maybe: "Where was God before Abraham?" Something like that. But Mom was taking a leap into prayer and answers. Where was she headed next? And how do I get out of this?

She turned a new corner. "I could ask you about your faith, son, but I won't. I might ask you—or anyone—what is your faith? Have you defined it? What do you believe ... who do you believe ... where is it taking you?" My Mom was up and kind of wandering the room, like she did when Colt was just a tiny thing. "I don't know, D, I really don't know. What do I believe?" She repeated: "What do I really believe? One thing. Just one thing." She stopped. "I guess what I believe is this. There's something greater than myself to believe in."

I shifted in my seat, wondering if she was near the end of this line of thought, when she added, "Well—one other thing. I know that we are all broken children.

"Daron—" I watched an eyelash flitter down from her face. "Daron—do you believe in yourself? Because it's okay if you do."

I weaseled out of a legitimate answer. "I don't know." Lame, but that was my answer.

"Like I said, it's okay if you believe in yourself. It's fine, really. No, I mean it—you're my son and I love you..." She drew in a breath and let it out slowly. "Really I do." Mom was tired, like she normally would be after a day of work. At night her shoulders pulled to the floor, and somehow life drained from her face. She lay down on the couch. She turned away, and I assumed she would fall asleep soon. I wondered if Mom fell asleep on the couch every night.

I headed quietly for the door. "Daron?" she said, turning my way. "When you do find your faith, just let me know. Okay?"

"Sure, Mom."

Then she said, "I love you, son." I had just experienced a talk about God with my mother. "I love you, too," I said, before stepping out into the dark.

CHAPTER 8

At the park the following day I did the usual scan to be sure no one spotted us. There were some little kids playing, but they were at a comfortable distance. We stashed our bicycles in some scraggly bushes.

Colt had his backpack loaded up, and that had turned out to be pretty useful. (He was going on about bringing "snacks" next time.) Of course I had the message envelope in my back pocket. Both of us carried some image of a real "Ilsa." Likely she was a white-haired woman of mystery who could call on visions. Well, anyway, a real person scribbled actual words on an envelope, for a reason. But the woman had died untold years or decades ago after preparing a note for a future recipient. And, good God, how did it end up stuck between books in this unheard-of place—that we were just entering? Did the same person also plant the blue ball? Why? Why did I keep asking these questions? It was speculation. A time-waster. Maybe there was no deep meaning at all.

"I have a message for you," was what Colt said when I told him about the Manninglys. Yeah. All we had to do now was sort through every detail of this debacle, including the envelope.

And—that voice that seemed to have a word for someone. For us. The back of my neck prickled every time I remembered that disembodied whisper. Now we were back inside and climbing the mile-high ladder to confront it again. It felt something like normal to reach the top level in a few minutes and see the home-base stack of books waiting. We had no plan other than to try to hear the voice again and walk a little, to see if anything was different.

Colt stepped on to the landing platform ahead of me. "Hey, Daron, do you think we'll get to ask questions and the voice will answer?" I almost jerked to a stop as another shiver hit my shoulders. I wasn't open to the idea of hearing "it" speak to me, much less answer my questions—all ten thousand of them. I just wanted a firm surface under my feet. There was no hidden corner in this open landscape of grass and clouds for a person or thing to hide, who might converse with two visitors from below. We stared at the familiar sky and felt air that didn't move.

"Mrs. Manningly," I said to no one in particular. It made as much sense as anything else if this woman's voice could be heard from beyond the grave. Or, that any "thing" could speak to us. Why me, or why Colt? Go talk to someone else, or keep your thoughts to yourself. "The Voice" didn't seem to be female or male. It was just a sound. We walked and looked around at familiar things. Colt bounced his ball. Nothing.

Walking away from the stack of books that marked our safe spot, we both noticed something that had changed or was changing in the distance: a slope. "Do you see that over there?" I asked. He nodded and pointed to the far-away spot. Was it a small hill? A change of landscape … the beginning of a rocky hillside? If so, then it may have grown up there overnight, and we would have to investigate. Colt bounced his ball again. We both heard it immediately. The Voice.

"Niles! I heard it! This time it said Niles! Who is Niles?"

No. Colt was wrong again. He didn't hear what I had heard. The word sounded to me something like "Style," which made no sense, because we needed more than one word. Not just a whispering murmur of sound that floated off to the clouds. Please, could we have more than just one word?

"Style." And it wasn't a female or male voice. Or, maybe it was, or even something in between. "Style" or "files" or "a while." What the hell. Maybe it was time to hear more than a word. "Colt," I said, "bounce your ball. Bounce it harder." There was a bounce, and there was the familiar hollow boom-echo from the distance. Bounce. Then we heard it, clearly. It was a new word.

"Always."

We stared at each other, with a new word buzzing our ears. On we walked, slowly toward that distant slope. The new word was as sharp as the blue up above. "Always." Now, finally, we had something new. She or he or "It" was speaking to Colt and to me in a tone as clear as crystal. Always? Always what?

"It wasn't Mrs. Manningly," said Colt, and I nodded. "Who do you think it is?" I asked. Then I added, "Two words, Colt. The first word was 'style' or Niles or something, and the other word was 'Always.' We need more words."

"It sounded more like a male voice, to me," he said. I shrugged. It sounded almost like a mechanical voice. Now we were even closer to the sloping ground but—no surprise—it wasn't really a slope because it went nowhere. Nothing more than a puzzle combined with a riddle and hooked up to a ruse. The ground started to climb up, but then it didn't because … I don't even know. We didn't know anything. We walked up but we walked down. No slope. But it looked like a slope. Colt bounced his blue ball.

"Always … Smile."

It shook me to my very soul. Every hair stood on end as I turned with a jerk and saw Colt's eyes glued to mine. I almost reached out to him to keep myself from falling. We both knew who it was.

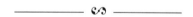

"DAD!!"

Colt hollered again and took off running. "Dad??" I watched him go. He ran toward the up-or-down slope which wasn't a slope. As he ran he didn't seem to be leaving me or diminishing but just running in place with small steps. I caught up with him simply by walking. I couldn't tell if he had tears in his eyes, but I sure as hell had tears in mine. Our father's voice, which we hadn't heard in over four years, was clear.

We stood and watched, and I wiped my eyes. Dad was not there, but we had heard him speak. I took the blue ball from Colt, looked at it and handed it back. He bounced it and we listened. "Always remember to smile," Dad said. It was his voice, and it was something he would say years ago, when we were much younger.

"Always remember to smile." My brother and I whispered, at the same moment:

"Dad?"

Why he used to say it, I really don't know. It was just a quirky thing about Dad that he would offer at random times. "Always remember to smile, boys," he would say. When things seemed to be going all to pieces or the worst possible news had been given, he still had that positive sound deep in his voice. Even when his diagnosis was death. Even when he knew he had only a few weeks to live. He was a playful soul at times. He could usually manage to smile for Mom or Rachael or Colt. Or me. There was joy in our father that must have come from—well—elsewhere.

Now he was here, wasn't he? It didn't matter what universe this was, it simply didn't make sense for him to suddenly appear out of nowhere with a soft, echoing voice. No, no—he wasn't here. Because nobody was here. When Colt bounced his ball again we heard it, and it was like a recording. The sound was identical each time. Awkwardly, I cleared my throat and said, again, "Dad?" There was no response.

Colt was sniffling and rubbing his eyes, and I reached out to touch him but he didn't look at me. "I don't get it," he cried. "We're here but Dad's not here. I don't get it." A sob shook him, and he looked at his ball. I wanted to say something and be the sensible one who could analyze, who could find answers.

"Bro, I am so completely lost. What does any of this mean? I have no clue, buddy."

Where do we turn now, who do we go to that knows the first thing about this forsaken place? There's a voice that used to be our

Dad. That's it. Nothing else. Nothing.

"This is CRAP!" My voice disappeared into the dead sky. "This is all crap! Get us out of here! Does anybody even care?" But there was no reason to ask or scream. It was just a nothing place. I turned him by the shoulder, and we walked toward our "exit," the stack of books. I reached for a cigarette in my pocket and remembered there weren't any. Crap. There was the sound behind me of the bouncing ball. "Always remember to smile."

He wiped away tears with the back of his hand. I sighed. "Let's go home, Colt." With the ball safely tucked away he eventually followed, after I began the descent. We made our way steadily down and down the long shaky ladder and felt sweet terra firma under our feet. It was then that Colt decided to mention something.

"There was somebody up there, D. Did you see her?"

I whirled around on him there in the book room. "COLT! Stop it now! You're imagining stuff again. There's nobody up there, and you know it. Not even Dad." I led him to the entry, my head throbbing. "We don't even belong there." I watched him slide open the hatch and once again, I was surprised by the brightness of day in the park.

"No, Daron, there was a lady. But I didn't think you saw her. After you got on the ladder." He watched me steadily. Under all that fluffy hair and oversized glasses his face was serious. "Listen. She's the Librarian and she asked about that stack of books at the top."

"Please, Colt. Just—"

"She said when are you going to return those books?" I couldn't think of an answer, standing there in a park with the distant sound of kids on the play equipment and moms yelling at their babies.

"Bro. What do you want me to say?"

"The Librarian asked me. So when are we going to return the books?"

Would anything ever make sense? I just wanted out of there. Please. And maybe I would never come back here again, maybe just stay home and read, listen to my record collection, and drink coffee.

"Colt. What-in-the-hell." Again, I felt in my empty pocket for a smoke. He was pointing his bike in the direction of home as I climbed onto mine. I yelled after him. "Right. You can tell 'the Librarian' next time she can have all her books back. If there ever is a next time."

"Okay, I'll tell her," he hollered as he pedaled off. "Her name is Mrs. Ell. I'll tell Mrs. Ell next time."

CHAPTER 9

Colt's new friend, "Mrs. Ell" or whatever he chose to name her, could have every freaking book in the whole dismal tower for all I cared. I knew there was no such person, but I might as well have said there was no such tall library with an echo of our Dad's voice. Pieces and parts of nothing, that's all it was. So, we continued our journeys up to the green lushness of the top level, to look for something but finding nothing. Only disappointment to take back home. I knew that Ilsa Manningly would never answer a single question about her message envelope or anything else. I knew that our Dad would never exist. I knew that I was more than ready for a final visit, so we could say a fond farewell to my brother's fevered dream world.

Colt was saying something about how this might be our last visit. I couldn't have agreed more. He was just ahead of me at the top level and was already looking around for something. Or someone. "Yeah," he went on, "maybe I really don't need to come back here anymore." If he was expecting someone, so was I. But it gave me the creeps, as always, having that feeling of eyes looking over my shoulder. Then he said, "She's not here, yet."

"Who's not here?"

"The Librarian. I call her Mrs. Ell, but that's not a real name. It's just the letter 'L'".

Right, I thought, that makes total sense like everything else. I had my eyes on the distance, maybe hoping to see something new. "Bro, you know just like I do there isn't any wrinkled old woman called The Librarian."

"No, she's not an old lady. She's real young and pretty." Oh, brother. Young! And pretty! Just what I needed to hear from this kid who knew special ways to annoy me.

"All right, man, if this pretty, young Librarian exists, why don't you ask her about Ilsa." He kept looking around, and I kept eyeing the horizon because there was something new and different. Maybe. "Do you see something over there?" I pointed. He shook his head and kept waiting and looking for her. But I was more interested in what looked like a tree. "Colt, over there: isn't there a tree standing way over there? One that wasn't there last time?"

He squinted, fiddling with his glasses, and then he nodded. "Oh, yeah. I see it! Let's check it out 'cause it looks pretty tall … but I want to talk to her first." He walked back over to the stack of books. "Hello, Mrs. Ell." He was talking to a ghost, a nobody. I couldn't make out what he was saying.

"Come on, Colt, ask your new friend something for me." I was smirking, but I couldn't help myself. "Ask her if she knows Mrs. 'M'. You know who I mean."

His voice was low, and it was a one-sided conversation with the Librarian. "She wants to know about these books. Are we done with them? Can we return them now?"

"Hell, yes! We're done with her freaking books!"

The "talk" went on. "Yes, we're done with the books now. Thank you." He chatted with his newest and dearest friend before turning back to me. "She doesn't know any Mrs. Manningly." Wonderful. And on it went, until—"But she said she does know about the message."

She what?? What in the name of holy—??

Colt continued, "Yeah. She knows about the envelope. I asked her why it was empty." He raised his hand as I started to interrupt. "Yeah, she said there was an envelope but it wasn't empty. But it was sealed." The hand went up again. "Hang on—"

I stuttered and fumbled for something to say. The envelope! We knew it was sealed and empty! But the invisible woman apparently had plenty to talk about. "It had a folded card inside, and it was sealed," he went on. "She's the one who stuck it between books." Oh, sweet Lord! What in the name of all that is just and kind was going on here?

"Colt, you asked her about it, didn't you? You asked about the envelope?"

He shook his head. "Huh-uh, all I did was ask about Mrs. M." The Librarian, our newest contact (who may have been visible only to 12-year-olds) had suddenly revealed more about the mystery message. The envelope was parked in my back pocket. I yanked it out for another look … as I had a thousand times before. Just inches from my face it appeared exactly the same. Wasn't it? Or, was there something there? Did I see the faintest outline of what may have been in the envelope, a card, folded? The more I stared, the more I wanted to convince myself. Yes, there was a slight outline or impression of its contents. What was no more—had left its mark.

Or, not. Because in the next moment I was as sure as ever that there was nothing to indicate any contents. Nothing to see or feel. But that tiny doubt lingered as I put it back in my pocket. Now, where had he wandered off to? "Colt?!" I saw he was headed toward the tree, and I followed.

We got there and found that it was a "tree" only in the barest sense of the word. Or, you might say, just another illusion. It was scraggly, scrawny and barely taller than Colt, with its two main branches spreading awkwardly to either side. What good was that? We were surrounded by green and the bluest of skies arched overhead, but here was a dead tree.

"I think I'm going to call this 'The GrandDad Tree,'" said Colt.

"What?"

"Yeah, it's the 'GrandDad' because it looks like it was here forever." He reached up for one of the two branches, and I flicked the opposite branch with my fingernail.

"Forever, Colt?" I laughed at the absurdity, and I heard my laugh echoing. "Yeah, exactly—except it wasn't here yesterday. But you go ahead. You call it the Christmas tree or the mighty oak or

'Grandfather,' if that makes any more sense than anything else."

"Let's go home," he said, then quickly turning back he said, "Bye, GrandDad Tree."

CHAPTER 10

Mom said she needed to talk to me, something about Rachael, so I headed over there on a Saturday morning. It turned out that our Sis had been calling with her usual load of crap for Mom, but now Rachael was "threatening" to come home. Ordinarily that could mean only one thing: she needed more money. To be precise, her boyfriend needed money. But, how many times before had she claimed to come home but never even showed up? I was about to voice my usual objection when Mom threw a monkey wrench into the center of my fuddled brain.

"Daron, next time you and Colt go to that Place—I want to go with you."

My eyes must have popped. I mumbled, "What—what place—do you mean?" I started to shiver, just hearing her bring it up.

"I know about it, and don't ask me how I know," she said. "You and Colt have been going to that 'Place' and I want to go with you." She gave me a steady stare that made me shift my eyes around the kitchen, but my head was in such a whirl that I didn't really see anything. I managed to squeak out something about "coffee?" Mom went to the counter and poured cold coffee into a mug, and I gulped it. She kept watching me, and it was that one sideways glare that tracked everything I did, like she used to do when I was about to get in trouble. I blew out a breath, like imaginary smoke. "Mom—" That's all I could say.

"We'll go together next time," she said.

"Mom." I still tried to put together a thought. "Mom, we can't take you there. To the—Place. Uh…" I continued, "Colt decided, I mean Colt and I, we decided not to go back. It's uh, not safe." Then it was her direct stare, followed by the inevitable, "Why?"

"How did you find out?!" I blurted. "I mean, really, it's not safe…"

Mom acted like she was going to get busy with some stuff piled in the sink. I watched her. If there had been a way for me to slither out I would have disappeared behind her back. All the weirdness of that fantasy world that Colt and I kept secret … but, she knew!

"It's something your Dad wanted me to know before he died." She turned, and there was the deep stare again. "I need to hear you say you'll never take Colt back to that Place again."

"Right!" I said. "Right, we're done! It's … it's too weird, and I just don't want to go back there, because…

"Because…" That's all I could say. Finally, I asked, "Mom, did you know we heard Dad's voice?" My own voice caught in my throat. She sighed, suddenly appearing weary, as she would at the end of a long day.

"Not exactly." She shook her head. "Not exactly… But it wouldn't surprise me, even now, to hear his voice." She stared again out the window as if waiting for someone. It was a moment when I felt she was drifting away from me, venturing deeper into her dark sadness.

A minute or so later she said, "I worry about him, you know." What did she mean by that? I kept my eyes on her back. "I worry about Colton," she continued, "because he gets himself mixed up in stuff like this. That's why I need you to watch him. All the time." I guess I wasn't sure how to do that, but I wanted her to know we were through having insane adventures. "I'll keep praying for you, both of you. I always do," she said. "I love you so much, Daron." Her eyes kept searching outside.

"Love you too, Mom." What else could I say?

CHAPTER 11

Late on Monday, as I was cleaning the bathroom and waiting to take some negatives out of the dryer box, it was kind of on my mind how there truly was a lot of love in this family. I suspected there was love between Mom and Rachael, in spite of their rocky history. Maybe we all loved each other more as a kind of tribute to Dad, because that's the kind of guy he was. And I was thinking how much I loved my little brother, even though he was a brat who seemed to find new ways to make me stab my eyes. As if on cue there was a message waiting when I stepped into the front office with a handful of negatives. Marie said, "Daron, there's a phone message from your brother."

Nothing would surprise me, but it seemed odd that he would be calling right after school. I picked up Marie's phone to listen. "Daron—I need to talk to you. This is Colt. You need to come over to the, you know, the Place. Meet me there, okay? Meet me in an hour. Okay, bye."

An hour? There was no way! I checked the time stamp on the phone display, and it said "3:35 p.m." Oh, crap. It would take me 15 minutes even if I ran to the park right at that moment. But I was supposed to meet the boss at closing time.

I saw that she was kind of giving me the quizzical look. "Hey, listen, Marie—do you think I could take off? I know the boss expects to see me at 5, but Colt needs to talk to me. I need to catch up with him, and it's been more than an hour."

She just smiled. "You go ahead—I'll re-schedule your meeting for tomorrow. Go on."

"Thanks!" I had all my stuff and was out the door in three minutes. I probably made record time jogging over to the old park, but he was nowhere in sight. Still catching my breath, I hollered weakly, "Colt!" Where was that kid? He wouldn't dare … would he? He wouldn't make me go in there by myself to check for him? I touched the "Mo SLAME!!" panel or door or whatever it was, and it gave easily as if someone had just passed through. "COLT!" No sound from inside that freaky place. I pushed a little more, and the panel rose into position. I peered into darkness and could see nor hear anything. "Colt, you better not be in here." I crawled inside and closed the hatch.

That silence: I'd never realized the dead quiet in there because Colt was usually rattling about something. After a few steps I hoped for nothing more than to get out of there, but I had to check further, where there was light. I thought I heard something, or did I?

I was in the library and he was not there, but I had a sense like something was breathing. It was a sound, like a teensy "whoosh." I looked up and saw nothing out of the ordinary. I started toward the ladder when I heard his voice, very remote: "Daron?" I stared up the ladder expecting to see him, but instead the ladder shuddered. And things started melting like film jammed up in a projector.

Again: "Daron!"

I still couldn't see him, but everything went into motion. I screamed, "Where are you?" Then I saw him, on the ladder and moving my way, but then he was gone because the ladder twisted itself. Shadows were dancing, finding their own altered states.

"COLT!" I started up the ladder, just hoping there would be steps for me to climb before it all shifted. What if I couldn't find him? My hands, wet and shaky on that ladder, clung tightly as my feet managed first one step then another. "Colt, get down here! Keep coming … can you hear me?" At first there was no answer, then a faint echo of his voice, calling. If things kept flipping and reversing up there I'd never reach him.

Then, with the greatest relief of my life so far, bit by bit I could see the overhead view gradually re-set itself as I saw my brother again, climbing downward. We scrambled down, and I grabbed his bony shoulders. "You little piss-ant!!" That was the best I could manage on short notice. "I'm gonna kill you if you ever do something like that again!" Then I reached and hugged him tight, hearing the beautiful sound of his rapid breathing. We held onto each other for a moment.

"Colt, you could have been lost up there ... what would I do if I couldn't find you?" He stood quietly, letting me hold him. "What would I tell Mom? I already told her we weren't going back here."

"I'm sorry." He managed not to cry, but it was an effort. "I'm sorry, D. I didn't mean it. You were supposed to come after I called you at work. I waited but then you didn't come. So I started climbing." He looked up at me. "I forgot."

But I was still furious. "We talked about this, didn't we? Never, ever go up there alone, only together." I looked into his brown eyes behind thick lenses, my fingers digging into his shoulders. "I'm just glad you're alive." I shook my head and gave him my best brotherly stare. "Now listen. This is it. This is our last time, and we're never coming back to this miserable place. Got it?" I was still trying to shake some sense into him.

"Got it," said Colt. "Okay, but, can we climb back up there now?"

"Again? Man, you just about died up there. You might have if I hadn't started climbing. What was it like?"

"It was scary, just like that other time. It felt like something was wagging me back and forth. All kinds of weird shapes and colors, and it kind of made me sick. Can we go back now and find Mrs. M's message?"

If I could have smacked him and kissed him at the same time, I would have. "What is the urgency all of a sudden? I thought we were supposed to be done with this place."

"But we're safe if we both climb the ladder," he said, pointing. "See? And I need to go up there because I know where it is. The folded card, you know?"

"Huh? What do you mean you know where it is?"

"The GrandDad Tree," he answered. "It's got to be there, I just know it. We just need to search all around there at the tree and we'll find the message."

"Lordy, Colt. We don't even know if that tree will be there, remember? How things are different when we go back there? We're not going to find it because there isn't any message." But I knew that any protest was pointless because all we had to do was start climbing again.

"We just need to try," he said, "and like you said, this is our last time. Let's go!" He looked up and then back at me. My aching head was telling me 'get this over with.' My heart was saying 'give the kid a chance.' Sure, why not—what's the worst that can happen? We could be dead.

"Bro, this is it. Last time."

He practically leapt on the ladder ahead of me, and I followed steadily. No turning back. Get it over and done with. The sections of books slid past us in waves. We reached the top in what seemed like no time at all. Colt passed our pile of books, and I joined him. There it was, the "GrandDad Tree" in the distance. What distance? On the winding paths the only thing I noticed was that the normally cheerful sky seemed slightly less shiny, or did I just imagine that? Colt ran to the tree while I walked slowly, arriving a moment later.

With its scrawny trunk and dual branches, the tree was the forlorn landmark in an empty wild patch of nothing. We began to search around its base, its branches and its faded bark for a clue that Colt seemed sure of. A folded card that should have been sealed away until found. "It's got to be around here," he said. "I think." But, it wasn't. Within minutes it was obvious that nothing could be stashed or casually left there for us to find. Nothing. Another waste of our time.

"Come on, Colt, let's head back." I started the short hike through the sometimes spongy, sometimes prickly grasses. But he wasn't ready to follow yet, and that was fine. Let him keep on looking for the card and maybe feel more useful. Something caught my eye on the way back—there was new growth coming out of the "ground" near the tree. The tiniest of trees, dark green, had popped up all around. Maybe they were some kind of Christmassy evergreens, growing just enough to poke up from the ground-cover. The tree spread out its sparse but protective branches as if to draw the tiny ones in.

Waiting for him, I decided to put away books. "Mrs. Ell" had never bothered to re-shelve our stack of books. Well, how could she? She had no hands. So I took it upon myself to put the books back— more or less—where I had found them on the top shelves. Starting with The Wizard of Oz, I slid it in an opening behind the polished railing. I re-shelved just about all from the stack, one by one. Ernest Hemingway, J. D. Salinger, Mother Teresa, Ray Bradbury, Gladys Carroll, Walter Miller Jr., Madeline L'Engle, Jonathan Swift, Charles Dickens, Anne Lamott, A. J. Cronin—I placed them all back where I found spaces, as I waited for Colt to finally give up.

I heard footsteps softly approaching. "No luck." He sounded defeated. "I guess it isn't there, anyway." I turned to see him ten yards away as I was about to replace a book by Nouwen. He stopped, mouth open, staring at me. "Daron," he called, "She—she's here. Do you feel it, D?" His feet froze to the trail. "Do you?" he asked. "She's here—"

"Who's here?" I asked. "The Librarian?"

"No." Colt didn't budge. "Mom's here…"

My brother. Was he losing his senses? Nobody was there, absolutely no one. "Knock it off, Colt. There's no one, just us. Come on, it's time to get out of here." As I turned to replace Henri Nouwen, somehow the book opened a little in my hands. Something slipped and fell out of the opened book and fluttered its little wings down to the floor. A card. A folded card lay at my feet.

"Mom's here!" yelled Colt.

It sent a shiver rushing down my back. Involuntarily I looked around, but there was nothing and no one except my brother running up to me. I stared down at the card which until now had been nothing but a flake of imagination. It felt like slow motion as I bent and retrieved it, turning it over to convince myself of the reality. It was a pale yellow folded card, about the size of a post card, and I flipped it over, again. "That's it!" Colt grabbed it from my hand. "You found it!"

The slow motion continued as I watched him open it. I heard myself mutter "I found it?" We saw handwriting inside, on both sides of the fold. Written on the left side were three words: "I Love You." It was our mother's handwriting. "Colt—" I said, and he interrupted: "Mom wrote this!" It was more real than almost anything we'd seen since starting this journey weeks ago. Our mother wrote "I Love You," and as Colt turned the card we saw what she wrote on the right side of the fold. She had written "Philippians 2:4-11." So it was that our newest clue was now in hand. How could it be more than all the other clues?

"I told you Mom was here!" My crazy brother was right, or I was as crazy as he was. "What's this about Phillipy? Is it the Bible?" I could feel that Mom's presence was somehow near although we were entirely alone. This wasn't the recorded echo of our Dad. This was real. But how could it be, unless she had been here? Was that possible, or was it even possible that Dad had somehow been to this nowhere Place? Colt was flipping the card over for any other detail.

"No … she couldn't have been," I said. "Colt, listen. This is getting real. I don't see how any of this makes sense, but listen: we have to get out of here. Now." I headed toward the ladder to start my descent. "Now, Colt!"

He hesitated. "Why the big hurry?"

"Because," I replied, "we have to make sure Mom is okay. Keep coming, fast!" I didn't even check behind me, but I knew he was on his way. Getting to Mom's was my new urgency, so why wasn't it for Colt? I hurried down to the bottom rung to wait, but those last rungs of the ladder were slow progress for him. One step down—then he waited, then took another step, with a longer pause each time. Waited for what? Those final 30 rungs were torture, and I bit my tongue to keep from screaming. Finally, he spoke. "I'm tired." Another pause, another step or two.

"I'll help you," I yelled, "just get down here!"

"I'm coming." He had stopped as if to view the latest Danielle Steele bestseller. Maybe five minutes later he stepped to the floor of the Library. I gave him the quick check-over, and he didn't look so good—pale and sweaty, with sleepy eyes. I did my best to help him along until we slid through the hatch and pushed it back down. Back in the bright of day, in the near-deserted old park where I played as a kid, he had a bit of energy. But it took a good twenty minutes to walk to the house, and I kept an eye on him the whole time. I made it to the door and knocked, then turned the knob. "Mom?" I called out, as Colt followed me in.

"She's not here." Rachael half-sat, half-lounged on the couch. Once upon a time a little girl with freckles played on that couch with her Little Pony. I was jolted, seeing her for the first time in more than a year.

CHAPTER 12

She looked older, although her eyes were as clear as ever. "Hi, Rachael," said Colt. "I'm going to go lie down." He headed off to his room. By then he looked just tired, not sick.

She was wearing old, faded corduroy pants and a t-shirt with some kind of bright zodiac design. Her feet, with orange-painted toenails, were bare and grimy. If I tried to describe her hair I'd say it was some kind of purpley-reddish. That's an improvement over the last time when it was black with streaks of silver and white.

"Rachael?" I said. "Where is Mom?"

"I don't know." I caught a whiff of stale cigarette, so I figured she'd been out smoking before we arrived. There was a People magazine open on the floor, and her Marlboros and lighter were on the coffee table.

"What do you mean, didn't she say where she was going?" I kept turning to check out the door. "Was she leaving for work?"

"She didn't say." She began to study her magazine.

It was a brother's duty to keep some kind of level opinion, but each time Rachael randomly called or showed up it pushed me farther into the dark. There was a pile of bricks between us, and I had to scale it just to see her again as flesh and blood. She did nothing to add warmth to any human contact between us. She was my little sister. I suppose I did love her. I also hated her.

"We have to find Mom."

"So, go find her." She avoided eye contact. "Good luck."

With my teeth gritted about to the point of fracturing, I got away from her. Mom couldn't be too far off, but where? Downtown? At Kroger's? At a bar? I half-ran, half-jogged and walked back toward the old park. My clenched stomach somehow told me she had tried to follow us there. What if something happened, she got stuck inside or something? There was a freaky world beyond that park, and anything could happen if you got lost.

I saw no sign of Mom or her old Accord. The old park was almost empty, as usual, but I pushed open the panel and hollered: "Mom! Are you in there? Mom?" Now it seemed unlikely, but was it possible she was there and took off already? She'd been thrown into the middle of Rachael's mess, so maybe she was trying to find some sanity, somewhere, somehow—or at least some quiet. Maybe even at the church, which was my next destination. I approached the old heavy doors expecting them to be unlocked, and they were. Inside, among the worn-down pews, somber crosses and colorful windows, I discovered a welcoming silence and peace. Or—worship? Is that what it was? No one was there. I felt a little out of place—it was my first time inside the sanctuary since Dad's funeral.

A sweet memory flashed across my brain, of his smile and cackling laugh. He shared his laugh with everybody, so why would I feel overlooked? Community college was my choice so I could "get away" from family and try to be on my own for more than a year. I guess it worked out all right as I learned my printing trade, and then I would come home for a break. There was Dad tinkering on some project in the garage, with Colt by his side. Or, there was Rachael returning from a long, meandering trek with Dad through the countryside. Hey, Daron—where've you been? Hey, Daron—what's new? Hey, Daron, long time no see. Time to eat, D!

Even after I returned from trying to find Mom, I was still mulling over that one quality about our Dad. Joyful ... is that what it was? By then I had covered all the places including the drug store and public library, and I was about done in. I found Colt, still sleeping it off. "Where's Mom, buddy?" He roused slowly when I shook him, and I asked him how he felt. Rachael, to no one's surprise, was gone.

"I'm okay. Where is everybody?"

"I don't know, man, I was hoping you could tell me something." Sis was not my priority at the moment, and there was even some slight comfort that she'd slipped away. We spent the next half-hour scrounging the kitchen for snacks and something to drink. Colt had two or three glasses of water. I managed to find a can of 7-Up, and we were eating peanuts in the shell when we heard voices. I hoped it was Mom and not Rachael. But there was Sis, puffing her Marlboro on the porch, and there was Mom, leaning against the far railing as if to avoid the second-hand. Out of habit I started to reach for a smoke, hesitated, and noticed Rachael's reaction—a smirk.

"Go ahead. Light up."

I ignored her. "Mom—I was out looking for you. Where were you?"

She kept her eyes on any movement in the street. "Oh, I was just driving, and you know, walking and looking at trees and such. Like we used to do, your Dad and I." (There: another "Dad moment" after my memory jolt at the church.) "Sorry, I didn't mean for you kids to be wondering about me."

Rachael spoke up. "No, we weren't worried."

I glared back at her. "What in hell do you know about it, Rache? Like you even care?" She looked steadily at me, a little gleam in her eye. That look could really set me off so I let her have it. "Why are you even here? Huh? You just show up with all your crap. You're here for what—to unload on Mom. You think she needs that?" Finches jostled in the bush nearby. Mom was the silent watcher, listener, as Rachael exhaled smoke. If only she could disappear into that cloud. I was not quite yelling. "Who brought you here?"

She smiled. "Alex dropped me off."

"Alex? Where is he now?"

Another smirk. "How would I know? Maybe he's gone?" She got in my face. "He's not here, is he?" Mom seemed out of it, with eyes half-closed. I wished for Colt to come outside or for anybody. A coldness crept up on me as I stared at Rachael, trying to come back with a retort. She saved me the trouble. "I'm going to see some friends," she said on her way back in the house.

A moment or two passed as I watched Mom breathing, her chest rising and falling as she swayed a little, the breeze lifting her hair. She seemed almost confused when she asked, "Where's Colton?" Just then he stepped out, and—for a minute at least—he didn't interrupt. I tried to think of something before Colt could start chattering. "Doesn't she have anything better to do with her life than—" Mom didn't react to my query, although I may have heard a little sigh.

"Yes," she said, "I pray for all my children."

What? It was almost as if she was answering a question. Her next words really rattled me as she leaned my way. "Daron, will you pray with me?"

Yikes—sure didn't see that one coming. Suddenly I was asked to join my mother in prayer, and I didn't know how, and I didn't know where. I looked around. Was anybody watching? Was I expected to make a move, like get down on my knees? To my huge relief I heard her say, "Oh, don't worry. I just mean will you pray when you think about it, sometime? Pray for me."

"Oh!" I gulped. "Sure, of course, Mom. I sure will." She went on, "You know, it's kind of like the mailman. We all just go on with our regular lives and our duties and routines. The mailman never stops delivering, and we hardly even notice."

We needed to ask Mom about the Place—and the card with her writing—and Dad. But she was rambling about mailmen. I had the odd feeling I was observing both of us from afar and trying to add some sense to the moment. There was so much we could have been talking about without the distraction of Rachael and her endless circus act. Colt must have been almost back to normal. "Mom!" he blurted, "We were at the Place today, and you were there! I mean, we saw your handwriting on the message." Typical, the way he could launch a thought that spewed from somewhere in that head. He blathered on, "I mean—we hoped you were there…"

For a moment she didn't react. Then: "No, I've never been there. Not inside, anyway." She sighed. Now it was my turn to stammer: "But—you said something about Dad, that he knew about the Place?"

"When I bounced my ball, we heard Dad." My brother appeared to be recovered, but I still wondered what had affected him.

"Rachael's ball," Mom said, with an eye on Colt.

"What?" Yet another smack to my skull—that memory! A toddler girl and her delight when we played "Roll the Ball" for hours, or at least that's the way it came back to me. Of course, I'd forgotten it was a blue ball. But, somehow it had found its way to the Place?

Mom watched Colt as if to connect with a long-ago voice. Maybe she was thinking what I was thinking, that Dad and Colt had almost identical vocal patterns. Her eyes focused near her feet. "Yes, he was there. Before he died. I don't know how. I just know that he managed somehow to find that Place." She spotted Rachael's belongings scattered around the porch and started piling them on a chair. "Rachael's leaving soon." Her voice was monotone.

Well... But our concern right then and there was how we saw Mom's handwriting on a card. If it was anything to do with the legendary Mrs. Manningly and her envelope, it might as well hang in the air like vapor and fade into nothing.

Her face softened. "It was a few weeks before he died, I think, that he said ... something..." We waited. "Something like—he wished we could be there, just the two of us. Somehow." I looked at Colt, then back at Mom. Her eyes darted this way, that way, up and down the street.

"You've never been in there—?" I started to say, "But..."

Rachael picked that moment to reappear and halt the conversation. She had changed into jeans and put on a baseball cap, her ponytail pulled through at the back. It was intense, that silence amongst us, and for about the hundredth time I was wondering how to escape a confrontation with my Sis. Mom was probably more hurt than angry about any argument they had earlier. Maybe I just needed to give them some space to figure it out, even if chances of that were pretty slim. I kissed Mom on the cheek as I stood up. "I'll be back later to see if Colt is still okay," I said, aiming a friendly bonk at the back of his head. I started walking.

Oh, Rachael. Let me count the ways:

Maybe I never totally figured you out, Sis, and you know I tried. Judging by the number of friends hanging around, you had to be the popular kid in school. I would come home and find a parade of people in and out the front door, and I didn't even recognize some of them. Loud kids, messy kids, rude girls … boys chasing after rude girls. What was the point? Shouldn't they have better things to do? There in the middle of it all was my sister, the ringmaster. Somebody had to be the one snapping her fingers and ruling over the funhouse, right?

But you still managed to make good grades, even straight A's during your 8th grade year, and school activities spilled over into our house with all the obnoxious kids. Then, when you demanded something from Mom and Dad it usually would be granted, mainly because Mom was just tired of all the pressure. When you had to stay an hour after classes in detention, it probably was a relief for Mom.

(She cut her own hair in 9th grade, and it was a chopped-off disaster. Oh, yes, after that she decided it was time for a self-tattoo. It's hard to fathom, but apparently she used the sharpened point of an old fountain pen, heated it, dipped it in ink and poked dots into her forearm. The result? Something that resembled an "R". Another disaster. Maybe all of this was high entertainment for Colt, but I worried that the nonsense would rub off on him.)

Rachael, you knew you could push Mom's buttons, and you pushed every single one. Then your grades were all over the place from 9th grade on. You sang the lead part in the annual musical-variety show, and people were shocked at your raw talent. "Almost Janis Joplin," somebody said. You locked yourself in your room for a day and a half, and when you came out you presented Mom and Dad with a homemade Valentine that included fingernail trimmings for decoration.

It was tiresome to see the parade of dirty clothes you wore or the shirts and jeans you shredded. But nothing seemed to slow down the social whirl with your friends … or your occasional disappearances. When you came home you'd all but fall down with remorse, begging Mom for forgiveness. (I felt sorry for Mom.) How long did your sentiment last? A day at the most?

You pushed me, too, Rache. You pushed me to the point where if I didn't get out of the house I might hurt somebody. I started looking for my own place and planning for college. But I still had to tolerate your girl-frenzies for more than a year, because there weren't any decent apartments I could afford. I couldn't stand to be near you, and I couldn't get away from you. Maybe I didn't handle all of it so well; maybe I could have adjusted my point of view so that you weren't the enemy. Maybe?

When I flipped out at your latest atrocious stunt, it just felt so right. Righteous. I guess it was a good vibe that lasted for an hour or so—that's how long I would feel superior. And, finally, I got away to my own apartment to celebrate my independence. Finally! It was a minor victory over the little harpy you had become. I felt sorry for Mom and Dad who were stuck with their wild child.

So, about the time I finally made my big move to independence, you quit school so you and that new pal, Alex, could start your new adventure out in the beyond. You left behind some broken hearts. Not the least of which was Colt's…

But let's not forget. Something else happened, the way things often develop, and it was "before Alex." Thanks to the sweet and kindly neighbor lady, one day Sis and her gang of friends moved their clan across the street to the ornate brick house on the corner, where the neighbor lived with her husband. He was gone most of the time, traveling for work, so she welcomed any and all young teenagers just to hang out. They felt at home when she invited them into her comfy kitchen or spilling out onto the veranda. Sometimes they were shooting baskets out on the driveway.

It finally dawned on me that they were doing some kind of unstructured church program or Bible study.

The kids and their adopted grandmother spread out with papers and books and maps and pencils and colorful charts to delve into some topic or teaching. They seemed to be having fun, drinking Cokes and having snacks. The quirky combination of hyper-active youngsters with a sweet and generous soul somehow clicked.

Rachael, you said the woman wasn't like any other adult. She simply opened her heart and home and kitchen table to kids who were drawn to her quiet influence. Later on, most of them would realize how she made a difference in their hectic lives. She was a friend and mentor and she made it look effortless. She was just there. If they needed a listener, she was there. If they needed to find their faith, she was there.

Or, maybe I should put it this way. It's entirely possible, even probable, that you and those kids in the midst of all your chaos found a little sliver of what you needed. What we all need…

Peace.

CHAPTER 13

I was no more than a few steps down the street when I heard her voice: "You leaving?" I looked up. "Yeah. Looks that way, doesn't it?"

"Let me walk with you. You weren't even going to say good-bye?" She was by my side as I gave her the silent stare. I kept walking. Suddenly she felt like talking? "What's up, Rachael?" I said. "I thought you had friends waiting for you, or something."

Her eyes met mine, and that made me uncomfortable. "My friends will be there later. I wanted to walk with you. Is that so terrible?"

"I'm going home. What about your boyfriend?" That brought a silence as we walked. Maybe I shouldn't have mentioned him.

"He can take care of himself," was all she said, and then she added, "So, if you were going to your place, how come you're headed to the old park?"

"No, I'm not." Was I? I whipped another glance at her. The ball cap didn't prevent her silky, purple-y hair from swishing side to side. "You don't know where I'm going," was all I could say.

"But, I just want to go with you," she said. Sure enough, our steps took us back toward that familiar Place—the home of all confusion. "Daron, you must think I'm oblivious." She turned when we saw the old stone footbridge ahead. "You may not know everything about me, but I know you're pissed at me. Mom's pissed, everybody's pissed at me."

I halted. "You can't be that clueless, can you? Are you here, or are you gone? You expect us to say 'All is forgiven'?" My hands waved my exasperation. "How about giving us a break, especially Mom."

Rachael was looking at the bridge. "I wanted to be here with you, D. I know all about this Place and you and Colton."

"No, you don't. Not unless Mom told you."

She smiled my way, but it was just a half-smile. "Listen to me—for once just chill out, so I can tell you. Dad knew all about it, all right? Dad brought me here. I know all about the Manninglys and the message and everything. I helped at their house when I was in junior high, taking care of their dogs when they were gone." I started to interrupt. "Listen!" she said, "I even cleaned their house later on. Old Mrs. Manningly was so sweet." She paused. "I think she kind of liked me."

I turned away from my sister as if to leave her there. Maybe if I went through the doorway, she would take a hint and get lost. Of course, that was not happening. What was there to say—that she and Dad kept this all a secret for years, and I was supposed to accept that fantasy? "Rache—" I paused because I thought she would speak up. "How are we supposed to believe you? Do you even know what truth is?" She exhaled smoke in my face and crushed out the butt.

I turned. My hands raised, I almost balled them into fists. "Rachael, you just don't get it. Here's a thought: why don't you just haul yourself back wherever you came from? Huh? Take your drama-queen act and your money-grubbing and your—" Her answer was to push through the little portal and leave me there, spitting and sputtering through clenched teeth.

"Wait—" I only hesitated a moment, then followed. How unreal, as my sister led the way and started up the ladder like it was an everyday event. My turn? As I had so many times through the odd assortments of books on all sides, I was now climbing and thinking of all those explorations with Colt. Somehow this didn't feel right. She was near the top, not even out of breath, and I struggled to catch up. Then somewhere below us, a voice: "Daron? Rachael? Wait up!"

Good God, could this really be happening? "Colt?" I yelled. "Dammit!" Now it was three of us on the jittery ladder, but Rachael cleared the top rung. Colt was catching up with all his usual energy, as I waited and wondered about his earlier weakness. Cursing him out seemed like the thing to do, but all I could manage was "You little worm!" We finished those final steps as Rachael waited. Sibling anger boiled up, and the only reason I didn't backhand him across the cheek was Rachael, smiling. "It's okay, I told him to meet us here."

I stared at them. When Mom found out about all this, well— things just might turn pretty ugly. "YOU told him!" I spat. "You know Mom's going to kill us, don't you?" I turned to Colt but he was already running toward the perimeter, with Rache following.

She raised her hands. "Look, it's so beautiful here!"

I slowly joined their trek. She seemed right at home as our little family of three tramped the friendly pathways under a magnificent sky. Dad wasn't there, physically, but somehow he might not have been far away. Something inside me started to seep through. A calmness? "What do you have in mind, Rachael?" My words tumbled out and fell flat into soft, curly grasses.

"Oh, not much." Her path took her toward the GrandDad Tree but Colt was jogging off in any direction that enticed him. "You know," I said, "we didn't find anything at the tree. The message we found was tucked into one of the books. Mom wrote it."

She quietly approached the tree like she expected to find something and began inspecting it from all angles. I knew, and Colt knew, that our search had turned up nothing. But my sister was intent on searching that lonely, dead tree. I focused more around the funny little tree-sprouts near the base of the tree, one of which, it appeared, was turning brown or dying. Colt was just trotting up to join us. Rachael circled around and looked at us, and then my eye caught something sparkling in the undergrowth.

"Look!" shouted Colt, and just then Rachael pointed and said, "There it is!" I thought something was shining up at me from between the grass blades—but, no, it couldn't have been. Could it? Colt watched as our Sis reached to pick it up, and it gleamed there in her small palm: a gold ring.

CHAPTER 14

She said, simply, "It's Mom's ring."

It didn't jump out of her hand; it didn't flash green and blue. The gold ring, simple and unadorned, just lay there like it had found its way home. My questions piled up like they always did when the mystery grew, starting with, "What—how could her ring be up here? Doesn't she wear this, I mean…?"

"I brought it here, but I guess it may have fallen out of the tree," she said. Colt reached out to touch the ring.

Did she just confirm her visit with (or without) Dad? Maybe someone who had connection with the truth could be believed, but this? This was my lying sister. Facts were zipping around my brain like gnats, and I wanted to swat at them. "Rachael, no, you couldn't have been here by yourself because—"

"I did," she insisted. "I climbed up with the ring because Dad would have wanted me to." We needed more detail than that, much more. Colt was itching to hold the treasure, and she handed it to him. Calmly, deliberately, she explained: "Right after Dad died, Mom said she needed me to take care of her ring. To slip it inside his casket, that's what she asked me to do. Somehow that made sense to her, I guess, that her wedding ring should go with Dad." The tear that hovered in her eye nearly trickled down. "But Mom couldn't bring herself to put it in there. So I took the ring."

Then why, I wondered, did a ring that was supposed to be buried with Dad end up here, on this surreal turf? "Rachael?" said Colt, "you—"

She interrupted. "But I just couldn't. So I let her down. I just couldn't tuck it inside the casket where it would be buried forever." Another tear formed in that warm brown eye and managed to find a way down her cheek. "See, it's here with Dad because he's here." Mom's gold ring. Rachael plucked it out of Colt's hand and carefully placed it back into the cleft formed by the tree-branch and trunk. "This is where it should be."

"But, wait a minute," I said, "the tree wasn't even here—" Colt burst in: "Yeah, we were the first to see it!"

"Nope," she said. "But I know what you mean. It wasn't there for me at first, either." A small grin lightened her sad face. "Then it just sort of appeared…" With wandering eyes she searched for details out there, somewhere.

"Dad loved this place so much. For some reason."

Then: "You know how Dad was…"

"Rache," I said, "I have to ask about climbing the ladder. We figured the only way to be safe was with two on the ladder at the same time. But, you came up here by yourself after Dad died?" Colt, almost as if he was losing interest, wandered away and sprawled down in the midst of little bright green trees, so we went over to join him. "Yeah," said Rachael, "I didn't have any problems on the ladder." This was weird, like everything else. I wondered—but not aloud—if a female was safe while climbing where a male wouldn't be, alone.

"D—" she said, "I'm just glad you and Colt finally made it up here." There was a sweetness and roundness to her face. Had I never noticed before? As we wandered among the welcoming grasses and mini-trees, the glint of gold from Mom's ring shone from its little niche, held by the lonesome GrandDad Tree.

—————— ✸ ——————

They had started calling me "D" way back when Colt was still put-
ting words and phrases together. It was the only shorthand that anybody used for my name. But there was a time when nicknames really
caught on.

"Birdbreath!" That was his name for her, so many years ago.
Rachael, of course, was still at home, and she had started calling him
"Nutball!" for some reason unknown to anyone else. So he came back
with "Birdbreath," and you could see how much fun it was to have
their special names. Maybe I didn't realize how often they played
together when Colt was really small or how much they just hung
out. I would see them, sometimes, all out of breath after running
or chasing each other around the block. They would hang by their
knees from a tree limb until they dropped, to see who could hang
longer or which one would land on their feet.

The only nickname for me was "D," and I don't remember
which one started calling me that before it caught on, even with
Mom and Dad.

Nutball and Birdbreath loved to play board games. The hours
they would sprawl on the floor with Sorry! or Monopoly or Trouble!
games spread out between them, and all the parts and pieces scattered around. They played Boggle or Scrabble when Colt was a little
older and able to assemble words from random letters.

"Hey, Birdbreath, what game are you getting me for Christmas?"
When I heard him ask her that, I gave them a Backgammon set. They
learned it quickly and it was their new favorite game. Watching them
together was kind of sweet, I guess. Then Colt grew into a fanatic
about reading, so we'd always see him with a book in his hands. His
favorites were wilderness treks and science fiction. Rachael was the
opposite. She was too busy to read. But I remember the many times
they sat together on the couch, and Colt's nose was deep into his
latest story, and she just watched him, stroking his head through that
wild mop of hair.

Later, maybe they drifted apart a little because Rachael wanted to
hang around with boys or her group of friends. For whatever reason

those quirky nicknames faded into memories. Even then I could see the friendship between them, when they'd walk home together carrying full bags of groceries from Kroger's. Or, when Rachael would make sure Colt got home safely from school when he had to stay for a club meeting and it started getting dark.

So it wasn't "Nutball" and "Birdbreath" any more, but they called me "D"—which was perfectly comfortable. And the label stuck. When I think back to how silly those two kids were, I wonder why anyone would use such ridiculous names. Maybe it served a purpose as kind of a secret identity between sister and brother.

CHAPTER 15

"I miss Dad," said Colt. "Sometimes we hear him when I bounce the ball." He linked his fingers behind his head, with his backpack as a pillow. Rachael, eyes closed and breathing with that little raspy noise, seemed distant.

"Mom figured this all out because she knew Mrs. Manningly, too. But, Dad was friends with her even before he met Mom. That's how they cooked this whole thing up." By "this whole thing," I figured she meant this "Place" of weirdness and questions, now holding us with its harsh beauty.

"Was Mrs. M some kind of—?" I didn't know how to finish my question.

"Mystical genius?" She answered with a smile. "Yeah, more or less. You could tell she had something special, even back then. She still does." I jolted upright. Another bomb had just been thrown. "What, Rachael?! What did you mean by that?"

"Oh, yeah," she said. "She's still around. You probably know her as Renda Fleury."

Holy moley! Someday, somehow, it would all make sense. But even now I would admit that I'd wondered if Mrs. M might be a living being. Rachael went on to explain that after Emery died, the younger Mrs. M went back to her maiden name, Fleury. Were there any other pieces dropping into place about the shiny lady in the big house?

Fleury the Mystic, maker of a place of contemplation out of nothingness for Dad and his family to enjoy … Colton, the "explorer" of our family with the knack for finding mystery right in the center of the ordinary? Even a non-genius like me might stumble into elusive facts now and then. Apparently all this was less than thrilling for Colt, who was snoring.

"This Place has always been here," she was saying. "Mrs. Fleury just turned on a light for us to see it, too."

I examined my sister: wild hair, dreamy eyes, air of superiority. "Dad wanted you to be here first," I said. Rachael replied with a nod: "Remember, you were gone to community college. But he wanted both of you here, too, before he got sick."

"Yeah," I continued, "Okay. But you said you knew about the message, but Mom said she didn't write it."

With that same little nod, she said, "I wrote it. Don't you remember when I used to practice Mom's handwriting, so I could forge messages to school? I did it all the time. I got really good at her handwriting." Rache told how she brought the message here after the younger Mrs. M gave her Ilsa's envelope.

"And believe it or not, I gave it to the Librarian." Well! There she was again, the invisible Librarian. I didn't ask how this curious being could remove a card from its sealed envelope, which was inscribed by Mrs. M. Did I really need to know how?

"You know that verse, don't you, from Philippians 2?" she asked. "Didn't you learn it like I did?" I shook my head. "Oh—I remember now—it was when our group hung out with Mrs. Q. You know?"

I nodded, even if I didn't recognize the neighbor woman's name as "Mrs. Q". "Anyway," she went on, "each one of us picked our own verse for memorizing, and I can still recite the first part. The part about Jesus: '...being in very nature God, did not consider equality with God something to be used to his own advantage; rather, he made himself nothing by taking the very nature of a servant, being made in human likeness. And being found in appearance as a man, he humbled himself by becoming obedient to death—even death on a cross.'"* Her words flowed naturally.

She paused. "Yep, I still remember. That, along with Psalm 100." Rachael's ability to make the connection stunned me, mainly because I never even tried to get interested in the Bible. "No big deal," she said, "but I know Mom tried to get my attention about her faith. Then, I just had to get away from her." There was a tiny sigh. "But I remember. And she wanted me to know that the Bible and church were about three things. Love. Forgiveness. And joy." She covered her eyes with her palms, as if to push the tears back in.

Three things ... but, it couldn't be that simple. Could it? My sister, who was not to be trusted, may or may not have been an expert on "joy." Wisely, I decided not to question her about her faith. Or mine. I could see, though, she knew something about love. That's how much she loved our Dad, and that's what brought her back here even after he was gone.

"Always remember to smile." Those words kind of spilled out of my mouth, and now she wept noisily with her head to the ground. "I miss—him—so much," she sobbed. I should have responded with a hug or something, but at least I reached out to touch her shoulder. She choked between sobs. "You know, D, I knew I had to get back home somehow and see you. Well, all of you." She used the sleeve of her t-shirt to wipe her face and nose. "It's just so damn hard. You know? But I made it here anyway."

"Who's crying?" said Colt, rousing from sleep. "Oh. Hi, Rachael." That brought a smile.

"Man," I said, "nobody can sleep like you can. Are you sure you're feeling better?" He nodded. "We were just talking about the Bible and stuff."

He stared with that drowsy look, then got up to go and take a peek and make sure the ring was still held securely by the tree. "I call it the GrandDad Tree," he told her when he returned. "But what it is, really, is the Cross."

*(Philippians 2:6-8)

—————— ❧ ——————

"Wait—what?" We watched Colt's feet follow the path, seeking who-knows-what. "What did he just say?"

"Oh, come on, Daron! Wake up!" she said with a flip of her ponytail. Once again Rachael was staring me down, but somehow the message eluded me. She waited.

"But," I said, "I don't see—"

"Don't be clueless, D. Look around. It's a Cross. And guess what—it's just for you." She pointed his direction. "And it's for kids like Colt, because they have faith."

Were they right? I did look around and there weren't any neon signs, and I didn't see any arrows pointing or yellow Post-it Notes with scrawled words on them. Instead, there was a battered Tree, and it reached out for me. My brother had just casually identified something for me that only a child could grasp. Rachael looked back at me with her sly little grin. "Didn't Mom say something about how Colt gets right to the heart of the matter?"

Was I "clueless"? My response to her was a quick and audible sigh that almost surprised me. And then, as we walked side by side, there was that topic that I almost didn't mention. Almost.

"Rachael," I blurted out, turning her direction, "something I try to understand, I guess, is how you and Mom have this continuing hassle—"

"No! Don't ask me. I'm not even going to talk about it."

"But," I tried again, "Mom said—"

"NO, Daron! Drop it! You don't even know the hell I've been through for the last year-and-a-half. YOU have no idea." She was getting in my face again. "Just leave it! I mean it." So much for me trying to help reconcile these two women in my life. So much for good intentions. Of course, I gave it one more try. "Rache—" She walked away.

Colt, moving her way, quickly wrapped her in a bear hug, and now she was weeping again. What was it with this girl? "Don't cry, Sis," he said. Meekly, I followed behind as the wandering paths led us in crazy directions. Again, we arrived nowhere because even the "edge" of this little world wasn't an edge. Every step, every move only brought us back to all the steps. Each movement was nothing but familiar from all we had done before.

"You know—" I began, cautiously, "I was remembering Dad's funeral and all those people packed into the sanctuary. Just looking at them, I knew at least half of them didn't even know what religion is or why they were in a church at all." (I didn't have to mention that I certainly belonged to the same group.)

Rachael, holding Colt's hand as they walked, simply nodded. I added, "So, what is the point?"

"Ask Mom," she said quietly.

I was puzzled. "Ask her what?"

"I don't know, maybe ask her if faith is real." But—even if I did ask her, I wondered, would "The Truth" sink in? Maybe Rachael was on to something. She added, "Maybe you could read Psalm 100 once in a while."

I worked up a little courage to offer something positive: "Rache, I know you're trying … to be nice…" By then we'd circled the Tree again, and Rachael slowed down. It seemed like she had more to add but hesitated with her thoughts. She halted. Finally, she said simply: "I'm never going back to him. I'm never going back with Alex."

Well. I cleared my throat. That seemed like a topic to avoid. So the three of us walked on, and again I noticed a miniature tree or two whose bright green had lost some color. I normally felt an urgency to leave this Place, and this time I tried to direct my brother and sister toward the ladder. We were headed that way, but Rachael hung back at the Tree. She said something about "checking Mom's ring one more time."

Then as I walked with Colt, she called out, "Hey, did you notice the moon is full?"

What moon? There above our heads was something I'd never noticed. Through the unmoving clouds was a full moon in all its glorious perfection. This Place never let up on its surprises. "See," she said placidly, "there's always hope." The light shimmered like never before and the moon, fat and full, added a feeling of impending night. "Colt—" I said, "was that there before?" He shrugged.

I looked back at my sister under that cool moonlight, and she appeared smaller next to the GrandDad Tree. The next time I paused to glance back she appeared tiny, thanks to the odd perspectives of this Place. I marveled at this strange point of view as Colt walked on. Rachael looked small even next to that ancient Tree. It made the Tree seem larger. The Tree was growing? How could it? "Colt, hang on a minute," I said.

During the few seconds it took me to jog over there my heart started to swell, and my head pounded. Something was suddenly very, very wrong. I wanted the perspective to adjust, for the Tree and Rachael to be normal size, but that didn't happen. "Rachael!" She was there but she wasn't there as I ran. She looked at me. The Tree was normal, but my sister shrank away from me. She stared into me as she diminished or drifted or melted away. Where? "RACHAEL!" Colt was screaming behind me. Her tiny former self was surrounded by greyish mist that tantalized. Her little image simply locked eyes with mine and then … vanished.

CHAPTER 16

Gone.

Colt rushed past me, but I matched his speed in an instant. The Tree stood solemnly where Rachael had gazed at the ring and faded away. This was impossible—no other tree or rock or corner could have concealed her. "Colt, Colt! Do you see her?" He chased after his own shadow, spinning like a top and looking, and I threw myself into empty spaces in the sudden desperation that she might be hiding. "No! Rachael?" Would she do something like that? Please, I prayed, please, please, please. Be there, just be there. "NO NO NO…"

"Is she gone? Rachael!" Colt cried. "Where? How?" His feet tangled and he tumbled down. I clutched my head to keep it from exploding. She was gone. The open landscape swallowed her. Where? Nowhere to turn. "Colt," I screamed, "we gotta split up! Search everywhere. Go!" He took off and I ran the opposite way, to the borderless perimeter where there was no start or finish, where you met yourself coming and going. "Rachael! Rachael!" Every scream and cry fell like a thud. "Rachael!" We searched. Nothing.

Sis. Baby sister. Sweet Rache. Where … how … please, please, please come back. Lord help us. What do we do? Colt collapsed, crying helplessly. I choked for breath and vomited. I could only stumble as I reversed course. There, is she there? Empty. Nothing but emptiness.

No, please, no. My soul was empty.

My feet dragged, and I made it back to the Tree somehow, and I circled it one slow, final time. Then, on my knees. Behind my eyelids weird colors flashed like bizarre Hallmark cards, fluttering. Rachael—gone. I almost forgot to breathe. I looked for Colt. COLT!! I screamed his name and he was there behind me, and I weakly reached for him as he flopped next to me. Lost. She was lost.

Mom. What do we tell our Mom when we return from this freakish Place with its shiny moon? "Daron?" He seemed to gulp for air. "What happened? Is she gone? Really?"

"How can she be?" was all I could muster. "…But we saw her go."
"We searched everywhere…"

I looked back at him. "We have to look again." It gave me no hope.
"D, I want to go home."

"So do I." I wiped my face against my shoulder and hugged my brother. Then the last search—slowly, methodically, to the edge and back, and finally, empty. We looked at each other by the Tree. Something like a silent fog settled and wrapped around us, invisibly. Our ears burned to hear her voice or anything—a twig snap, a leaf fall. The moon burned even brighter, and with that light we could still see a few little trees turning brown or dying. We waited.

"We're leaving," I said. Now it was growing darker but with the pure, intense light of a full moon. "I'm scared," he whispered. Our shoes left the merest impressions as we rustled through the undergrowth. Night was falling. The GrandDad Tree held its precious treasure: Mom's ring, glowing with the warmth of her hand.

"We have to tell Mom about Sis." A few strides away from the Tree I saw something caught below our feet in the strange grasses: her pack of Marlboros. With every ounce of force I could summon, I crushed the pack and ground it in so hard that my heel ached. We made it to the ladder. "Come on, Bro," I said, not even checking if he followed. Then, from behind: "Daron, do you think if—"

"COME ON!" My shriek echoed through the night.

The moon gave its light, enveloped in an open and limitless vault of blackness. We climbed down the library as we had so many times these last few weeks. We stopped at the bottom to look around. Slowly, we walked toward the doorway, and Colt hesitated. I turned to look back at the shadowy cave. "Man, I can't leave her." I felt his eyes on mine. "I have to go back—" And just as I stepped toward the light, everything changed.

The endless ladder? Gone. The books? Every last one vanished. We peered into a vacant room with just enough "moonlight." There was a ladder after all, an ordinary one, leaning up against a plain wall. It was Colt's turn to whisper into the silence: "Daron? Are we going to die?" I had no answer as we reached for the ladder, and he followed up as we climbed 10 rungs. I crawled over the edge of the wall. Colt breathed in my ear as we took in the sight: the Tree, which appeared taller than before, was bathed by the moon but all the rest had been erased—all except for a handful of the little green trees. About half of them were fading.

No familiar landscape. No clouds, no stars in that dark canopy, only a moon. And there was the faintest moon-pierced glint of Mom's ring. We held onto each other, shaking, longing for the comfort of a familiar face. I felt the gush of tears coming out of me, soaking his hair.

I would have crumbled into a pile on the ground … but somehow my brother held me up. "Let's go tell her." We turned away from the Tree.

The hard brightness of day blasted our eyes after we squeezed through the hatch, which closed with a loud "thunk." Colt turned back to look and grabbed my arm. "D? Look…" The bold graffiti-painted letters on the hatch door were fading, disappearing. A blank surface remained. I knew we had to try so we both shoved as hard as we could, and it would not budge. There was no doorway.

In this world there is evil—that's what I believed. If I ever had opportunity to take this all apart, I'm fairly certain my sister was swept away from us not by evil but by something other-worldly.

How to put it into words? It was going to break Mom's heart, again. For decades she and Dad had a lovely relationship which had been torn in two. Now this. It would throw her into depression possibly even darker than four years ago.

It may have taken us longer than usual to walk home, partly due to Colt dragging his feet again, but mainly because of the ache I had for the moments to come. Behind us was the old park which no longer held any destination beyond the ordinary. Rachael was there … and then she wasn't. A person doesn't just vanish. Would we find her lying in a ditch somewhere?

Mom was still on the porch, but when I choked and said there was something we had to tell her, she immediately went inside. I can't remember what I said or how I managed more than two words. Silently, on the couch, she slowly leaned and her body slid down as if melting into the covering. We couldn't see her face. Colt's sniffling was the only sound as Mom's shoulders quivered. An image of Rachael came alive in my head and just as quickly faded and died.

"We'll call the police and get started searching for her," she said finally, her voice muffled and soft. It's just what I dreaded, for all the questions to be thrown at us and every answer to be concocted from our pit of sadness. Plus, knowing that every hour of seeking the lost Rachael would be an absolute waste. How could we explain to any of her friends or former teachers and acquaintances that they'd never see her again? This was different from all the other times Rachael wandered. At least then we had a shred of hope for her return, to be followed by her next disappearing act. Mom needed to grasp that Sis was really gone this time.

So it began. She was up and in the kitchen to call the police station, and a couple of minutes later they were knocking. The questions for me and for Colt were never-ending, but they all led to the old park. I kept saying to the police chief that he would have to see for himself and as soon as possible, and by the time he finally agreed, Mom was making sandwiches for everybody. We all grabbed one and climbed into the patrol cars. Colt stayed with Mom, who stood in the doorway as we drove off.

The top of the bridge was ground-zero, the place to start where we could see most of the park. How many times did I say "You're not going to find her here…"? It didn't matter because the police were going to be methodical no matter what. They were going to have a grid system back at the station for volunteers who wanted to do their part. The "grid" would over time expand well into the southern half of the county. And those well-meaning folks were going to flock to the park and beyond for their grid-search until Rachael was found safe, and they could claim credit for the rescue.

Except that wasn't going to be. "And you say you've checked the whole park?" the Chief said for about the third time. His head swiveled, and his eyes took in every lump of ground and crumbling sidewalk while the officers spread out. A sheriff's car drove in, and a deputy got out with his search dog to join the squad. From the old bridge we watched the buzz of activity. I didn't want to say another word after all the questioning—and when would they realize there would never be a trace of Rachael? Underneath was nothing but dirt and deep shadows.

The Chief was occupied with some detail with somebody so that, finally, I could slip away from the "search." All the way back to the house I met volunteers on their way to join the others. It was the biggest event in town for years. Mom was waiting inside, wearing one of the dresses she wears to work, with diagonal stripes in bold colors. I heard Colt rattling around in his room. Smoothing the bright fabric over her lap and folding her hands, Mom stared straight ahead. I loved her more in that moment than ever before. We sat together on the couch, close. I worried, again, about her strength now that one of her flesh-and-blood was missing and most likely dead.

"Mom, they don't have any idea what this is about. The Place, I mean. How could they? They—I mean, I just don't know who can make any kind of sense out of it." I added, aimlessly, "I mean why now? And why the Place?"

"There's a prayer I have for my children, and I pray it for you every day, and that's all I can do right now." She turned her soft smile toward me. "What do we really know? If we know any detail, it's about that Tree of Life." Her hair was drooping across her eye, and I reached over to brush it back into place. "We're broken, son. We're His children and we're broken. We're all going to die on that Tree."

Colt was still rummaging around so I went to check on him. "What's up, Bro?"

"I wanted to see if there's any gear I need when I go search." His voice filtered out from somewhere deep in his closet. He emerged with a floppy hat and a souvenir keychain with a miniature flashlight. If only I could have said something wise to Colt. If I could have made him laugh… "Bro," I offered, "maybe you don't need to go searching."

"I wanna help the police. I talked with Grill and Blink, and they're going to help."

If only I could have loved my brother more. Maybe I could have figured stuff out for him. "They have their grid assignment," he said. "I'm going over there with them." Ah yes, the "Grid" where all will be made tidy. I heard the phone ring, and Mom answered. I supposed it had been ringing all day.

"Colt," I said, "do you think somehow she's going to be out there?"

"Rachael knows how to take care of herself," was all he said. He picked up a piece of paper off his desk and showed me. A prayer was printed on it:

The light of God surrounds me.
The love of God enfolds me.
The power of God protects me.
The presence of God watches over me.
Wherever I am, God is. *

"Mom gave me this," he said. "It's her special prayer for Sis. I'm going to try to memorize it."

**"Prayer for Protection" by James D. Freeman*

CHAPTER 17

I was back with Mom when she told me, "Daron, your boss called."

Oh, hell yes, the boss. I'd forgotten I had a job. I kissed Mom good-bye and promised to check in. The rest of that day and all the days after seemed to be about working and seeking ... something. I pumped ink and loaded ink trays with black and colors. I did the annual inventory of paper supplies, envelopes, forms and chemicals. I wandered the town with all ages, shapes and sizes of my fellow citizens and church members who had plenty of puzzled looks for me. I scratched out order forms and handed them to John-the-Printer who couldn't quite decipher my handwriting. I joined Blink, Grill and Colt in their grid, now that school was out and each day was wide open. Several times I reached the city limits on my own and wandered around. Someone was missing but not to be found. We kept looking. The pastor called and took me out to lunch. We chatted and I thanked him.

I encountered Mrs. Fleury occasionally, and she was always so pleasant. Of all those out there searching for Rachael she seemed the most hopeful. Back at work, the Boss was nowhere to be seen. I tried to help Marie understand that a complex, perforated triplicate form was always a special order and had to have an extra week for completion. She and I talked briefly about "Renda." From what I could tell, nobody—not even Marie—had an idea of who or what Mrs. Fleury truly was.

Mom also was trying to recreate a routine, and I saw her several times at Kroger's. Any time I checked in with her she would have that soft smile for me, the one reminding me that I had the most patient Mom who ever lived. When I would see the officers around town they tried to appear efficient and busy, but I got the feeling they weren't sure what they were looking for or how long to keep up the pretense. I sure couldn't blame anybody, though, for any doubts they had about Rachael's disappearance, or "leaving town." After all, wasn't that what we all expected of her?

Some days Colt and I would walk together. Other times I'd find him wandering, but Bilder and Gregg were nowhere in sight. By then we were into the second week, and the number of people combing the streets and nearby fields was way down. I couldn't look at my brother without reading that deep futility in his sad eyes, and I wondered if his eyes reflected my own. How long would we all pretend that we'd ever find any trace of Rachael? So far, no one was saying anything about holding the memorial service. Not yet.

One time, I was catching up with Colt, and Mrs. F was walking with him. As I got closer I could hear her thin, mild voice singing. The haunting sound was some sort of ancient hymn or chant:

"The Lord's my Shepherd
I'll not want.
He makes me down to lie
In pastures green, he leadeth me
The quiet waters by.

"My soul he doth restore again
And me to walk doth make
Along the paths of righteousness
E'en for his own name's sake.

"Yea, thou I walk in death's dark vale
Yet will I fear none ill.
For thou art with me and thy rod
And staff me comfort still.

"A table thou hast furnished
In presence of my foes.
My head thou dost with oil anoint
And my cup overflows.

"Goodness and mercy, all my days,
Shall surely follow me.
And in God's house
Forever more,
My dwelling place shall be."*

*Taken from the Scottish Psalter © 1812, Crown & Covenant Publications. Used by permission.

The shiny lady's voice lifted and carried me, verse after verse. I couldn't tell if Colt was crying or not, but my vision was blurry and wet. As we walked on she was saying, "I wish I could say a word for you two young men that somehow would help you get through all this. I wish we could see God's love just flooding down on you and your sister." She motioned upward with her hands. "Never doubt that love is true, and please know that you are never alone, ever, nor is Rachael, through any step of this journey." Mrs. Fleury's lingering song resonated with me that day with soft, sweet, fluttery notes. For a moment at least, there was real comfort in her words.

And so we soldiered on. It was hard for us to see our Mom, day after day, slipping down into her deep sadness. She had stopped trying to go to work. Fortunately, neighbors and church folks kept bringing us food. When anyone said anything about Rachael or the folks looking for her, Mom didn't react. When she was sitting with us there wasn't much talk, and her eyes were often closed and her hands were in her lap. I didn't see her reading her Bible a lot, but it was always nearby. Once, staring out the window, she said, "Never take any sunset for granted." In her lined face Colt and I could see the painful loss of a child. But I thought I saw something else—a kind of peace.

Weeks passed. Mrs. Fleury stopped by the office one time, and I guessed she would be placing another order with Marie. Instead, she asked about me and if I was available. I returned to the front desk, and Marie more or less ordered me to go walking with Mrs. F, so we stepped out and walked through the downtown area. We continued on some of the streets and roads that had been scoured over and over by searchers, some of whom were still to be seen. She was talking to me about the Rachael I barely even remembered. "She was much younger then, but I know she really looked up to you, her big brother." This was a quick reminder of the bitterness I had tasted whenever the name "Rachael" came up. Maybe I wouldn't say the words to anyone, but I still carried the scars of the times my sister burned us and the times she hurt our mother.

We walked past storefronts and bungalows and vacant lots as I half-heartedly looked—for what? For who? I listened to Mrs. Fleury's kind and forgiving thoughts. She even talked about neighbors or people who had moved away or local politicians and clergy. You can find good in anyone, she was saying. "But it can be hard to find good in the people closest to you," she added.

I looked down at her walking boots. "I still love her." Those were my words, but who did I convince?

"Daron," she went on, "when we love the unlovable, we can smile once again in the mirror. Maybe that's just a small step. But for me—it comes back to faith. And sacrifice. Do you know about Communion?"

"Sure," I replied. "I guess." We had walked generally toward the neighborhood where she lived but didn't turn onto her road.

"Your mother and I have had many talks about it and about all of you. Jesus gave us the Cross. It's his greatest gift, and there are so many reasons that we need it. He also gave us Communion. It's the action of one Man for all the rest of us." We had halted our walk for a moment. "He freely gave that gift of his body and blood for me and for you and every individual who ever lived. We accept it but can never earn that gift."

There was a sadness in her voice. "It may have started with Abraham, but it was finished by Jesus Christ. My faith, your faith—it's always a struggle. It goes on inside you. Lots of prayers."

I had to ask her: "What about the Place?"

She sounded matter-of-fact. "I've never been there, I just know all about it from your Dad. He just needed a little help finding it. And, I gave the envelope to Rachael so she could leave a message for her Daddy." I had to look away. I didn't have the energy to run and I wish I could have, but my feet were anchored.

"Mrs. F, I know I'm supposed to pray ... for Rachael. I don't know how."

There was a small smile. "No one knows how. Nobody. We try to do the best we can, and he's listening anyway. You know, Jesus has some suggestions—you can try them. You'll be fine."

At the end of our walk back to the shop I thanked her and managed to ask, "What about Rachael?"

"I wish I knew," she said as she gripped my hand. "I just don't know the answers. But, Daron, remember this and please tell your brother: we will all see your sister and father again. You knew that already." I nodded. "And don't forget that someday you'll celebrate Communion, and there will be a quiet voice saying something like, 'I did this for you.'"

There was something that Mom rarely, if ever, mentioned, and that was the time of Dad's sudden "disappearance." She would smile and shake her head if the topic happened to come up. I know that they worked it out. They had an understanding. Part of it was that every year or so Dad needed to have some isolation, from everything and everybody. So, Mom was fine with it because she knew he would always return. Except—he almost didn't.

He would pack up his old pickup truck with some weekend supplies and a sleeping bag and a little food. He drove somewhere in the remote woods or to the end of an abandoned road. Or, near a creek where he could catch a fish or two. We didn't have a dog but if we'd had one, I'm sure the old mutt would have been along for the ride. Dad cooked his supper over a fire and watched the skies. Don't we all need a little time to wander off, just a day or two to gather some thoughts or look ahead? Then, maybe you feel like you've got your stuff together so that you can face people and be friendly again.

I was supposed to have gone with him that time, and that's why it feels so different. When I remember how it all turned out, and when I try to sort so many regrets—that's when I miss my Dad the most. I should have been there. It was supposed to be a guys' weekend instead of Dad's usual private escape. We were going to bring back a load of fish. I was barely eighteen. Maybe I didn't crave isolation back then, but it would have been a chance to feel closer to Dad's challenges and how he handled them.

At the last moment I backed out. Then, the girl I was supposed to meet that weekend didn't even bother to show up for our "blind date." A disaster. Because if I'd been with Dad instead, he might not have been lost. We didn't know where he was for more than a day. The sheriff didn't know about it, but Mom was almost ready to declare a missing-person. But—I said—Dad always returns. He'll be all right, for sure. "We just need to let him figure it all out," I said. We didn't know about the broken collar-bone.

This wasn't like Rachael's vanishing. Dad was Mister Capable, and he was the problem-solver of our little family. Here, he was facing one he couldn't quite handle. One of the rear wheels dropped over the edge of the road as he put the truck in reverse. It was wet and sloppy, so he had to try gently rocking forward and back without digging the wheel in deeper. The chain of events continued as he was climbing back in the truck cab and slipped in the wet muck, twisting and grabbing the open door as it closed on him. His shoulder wrenched against the truck as his feet slipped out from under. He heard the sound of cracking bone.

Somehow he managed to maneuver part of the way back to the main road but all that shifting around just multiplied the pain. He had to wait for hours hoping it would subside ... it was getting dark. Turning the steering wheel became impossible. He dozed in the truck overnight. A farmer heading out to his field saw the truck in the early morning light. Dad was rescued and hauled out of there hours later, and he was in the hospital before noon. "Always remember to smile!" he said as we were leaving his room. There's an intense kind of relief when someone you love turns out to be alive when he could have been dead.

This time? Things were going to be different. If you could excavate under the stone bridge in the old park for a week, would you find Rachael? Nothing. Maybe a few tree roots and here and there a rock or two, and more dirt. All blanketed under the unbroken grassy turf. Empty.

CHAPTER 18

There was nothing left to say. So, I continued to go through the motions at work, at home, and with Mom. She was the same, but I wondered if she'd ever say that Sis would never be seen again. The silence at the house was so ominous that I wished Colt would make some noise. I looked over Mom's shoulder to see what she was studying one time, and she had marked a section of Isaiah 61:

8 "For I, the LORD, love justice; I hate robbery and wrongdoing. In my faithfulness I will reward my people and make an everlasting covenant with them. Their descendants will be known among the nations and their offspring among the peoples. All who see them will acknowledge that they are a people the LORD has blessed.

"I delight greatly in the LORD; my soul rejoices in my God. For he has clothed me with garments of salvation and arrayed me in a robe of his righteousness, as a bridegroom adorns his head like a priest, and as a bride adorns herself with her jewels.

For as the soil makes the sprout come up and a garden causes seeds to grow, so the Sovereign LORD will make righteousness and praise spring up before all nations."*

*NIV (Isaiah 61:8-11)

John-the-printer had a day off to go fishing. His version of being "off" was to come in at 4 in the morning, run the press for a solid four-plus hours and disappear the rest of the day. I was dragging kegs of ink through the back door after the delivery guy left, and I just stopped. What was the point? I took off my smeared apron and walked out the back without a word to Marie or the boss or anyone. Was it dark that morning or was it just me? I watched the house finches and drank coffee on my front porch, but it was like acid going down my throat. A straggler walked by, and I mused that this could have been the very last hopeful searcher. What to do, join the throng? I crushed my cigarette—and as it turns out, that was my last smoke, ever.

My body said no, but I wandered out anyway to more or less follow the usual route. It took me back toward the edge of town where I knew I would reverse and head home and try to sleep it off. Oh, about that: I wasn't really sleeping any more. I would sit up at night and stare out the window. I'd roll around in bed, and no pillow provided any comfort so I threw them on the floor. Next to the bed was my Bible (the one they gave me for my 11th birthday), open to those last few verses of Matthew, Chapter 6. I planned to go back and read or study those lines again, someday.

Was I scraping pretty near the bottom? If I happened to dream, it was just an image over and over of Rachael staring blankly at me before evaporating.

We all knew the process was all but finished, and the "Grid" had served its noble purpose. One by one the searchers had realized there were other priorities. Maybe they had a calling or a higher goal. Something other than my sister, now that she was just a memory. Something prodded at me as I started my solitary trek: it was that time when I was still living at home, and I heard Rachael returning from a night with friends, drunk. Mom helped her through the door where she staggered until collapsing to the floor. She threw up. I saw Mom cradling her head, trying to smooth her hair back and reaching for something to clean up the mess. Rache was in Mom's lap and now ready to curl up for a nap, peaceful. Mom caressed her neck and forehead. There was never a word between them about that night, as far as I knew.

From the farm fields a bit of dust was swirling around, throwing grit in my eyes. I tried blinking it away but it still obscured my vision, or maybe it was that strange mist rising up from the wheat stubble like shimmering, grasping hands. I needed to get away from that advancing gray motion. Someone hollered. I turned, but saw no one in the mist. Perhaps it was only that wandering soul looking for my sister. There was another yell, and I turned at the moment a small figure emerged from the gray. He was running toward me. He charged right past me like I didn't exist. It was Grill, Colt's friend, and I heard him yell again.

Something fluttered in my chest, and it burned and spread through my shoulders. I may have stopped breathing. There was another running figure as the mist parted just enough to reveal Colt's other friend, Blink. It was my turn to run and I tried, but it was a dream and my feet could only lurch toward that wall of grayness. Blink was immediately followed by my brother, shouting. Nothing he screamed made any sense. "Colt!" I yelled. "Colt! What—?"

The parting of the mist continued, and a bit of light penetrated. Two figures gradually emerged.

CHAPTER 19

Renda Fleury Manningly was holding her hand as my sister slowly walked through that foggy dream. And then it was real. I didn't grab and squeeze Rachael with the fiercest hug ever observed, but I did hold her close to me to be sure she was alive. I didn't squall like a baby with tears drenching her neck, though I truly needed to. I kissed her then looked in her eyes and said her name, and then I had to turn away. I turned again and hugged Mrs. F and kissed her cheek, and I grabbed Colt with enough force to break a rib. "Hey!" he cried, so I let him go.

Someone was babbling. "It was just like in that movie about the lost baby, remember? And we thought we heard something but then we didn't. And the lady was there, but it was hard to see. I saw Rachael first, and then Gregg saw her and so did Bilder. Right, Blink? And… and…" The babbling went on. I took Rachael's hands in mine, felt her soft palms, and then I grabbed Mrs. Fleury's hand so we could head back into town, away from the clinging fog. My sister's steps were labored but I didn't see any stumbling.

It still felt like a slow-motion daydream. By the time we got to the house, Grill was catching up with us after waving down the first cop he found on Main Street. He flopped on the step and tried to breathe. We heard a patrol car's siren in the distance as Colt brought Mom outside. Our mother may have been even more unsteady than Rachael, but with clear eyes she took in the sight. Slowly, Rache approached Mom and they embraced. The hug was long enough that I worried for their stamina until, finally, they sat down together. My face was wet, and I tried to wipe it off. Rachael leaned against Mom and, somehow, she melted into her as Mom's shoulder became her pillow. Rachael was home.

I stared. Was this the same sister with the same goofball hair and skinny jeans, the same pale skin? No doubt she was tired, and her eyes flicked here and there before returning to familiar faces. She smiled. If I hadn't seen that smile I might have doubted her return. It felt like the smile was just for me. I saw a smudge of dirt on her neck, and her shoulders were sweaty. Mom kissed her and patted her back. "Where have you been?" There in the shade of our front porch, we waited.

She sighed. Her mystery began to fade, but there were so many questions. "Are you hungry?" Mom asked, and Rachael nodded. "It was kind of light, and I wasn't scared." Chattering sparrows nearby seemed to hush and wait for her to tell a story. "Sometimes it was dark."

"You were in the Place, right?" asked Colt. "But it's all gone now." "No."

The puzzles and facts to be unraveled felt like a headache. How could she survive, and how did she find her way back? She waited patiently, and I tried to calm my jittery feet and hands. It was then I noticed her ball cap was missing, and her hair draped over one shoulder. "No," said Rachael, "it was something new and different, just a kind of lightness and then shadows. I just kept going because I needed to find somebody. I kept looking for Mom and you guys." She reached over to Colt and gave him a squeeze. "I must have wandered for at least a day. Maybe more." Her eyes closed.

"Rache," I mumbled as the police chief got out of his car. "Rache— You've been gone three weeks."

If she was stunned by that fact she didn't show it. There was another little sigh, and she paused as if to gather more thoughts. The Chief took over at that moment. For the next half-hour it was one uncomfortable question after another. I wanted him gone but the man persisted even as the sweat dribbled down his back, and he took notes so he could type up his report. All questions were asked, and nothing was revealed. When he left he was a bit dazzled.

Others were coming by as word spread through our little town, so that at one point there was quite the audience to see the "missing girl" at home. It's a good thing the pastor showed up and started convincing the herd to move on so we could have our time of reunion. Before he left we all held hands, and he praised God for her safe return.

"I just don't know." Rachael paused to gulp more of the water that Colt handed her. "It was weird. I remember at first you and Daron were there, and you were both fading away until you were gone. There wasn't any noise. I knew I had to find you, so I sort of wandered around. If there was a shadow I just kind of pushed through it to the other side." She again half-closed her eyes, and there was such a long moment that she appeared to doze.

Colt blurted, "Was God there?" I stifled a laugh, and Rachael flashed a lovely smile.

"No. Well—yes. Was it God who watched me?" She seemed to try and read Colt's eyes with that special connection of theirs. "Yes! Because even in those dark areas I never felt alone. Or, even lost."

"What about Dad?" he persisted.

"Well…" We waited. "Yes. I mean, it was the strangest thing. I saw something: it was a chair. Nothing else. So I went and I touched it, sort of put my hands on the back of it like this, and that's when I knew. Dad was in that chair." She blinked as a little mist floated over her eyes. "Dad was sitting right there, and he wanted me to know I was going to be all right. No, I didn't see him." Another pause. "He was there."

Colt jumped in again: "But—"

She almost laughed. "He really wants us all to know!"

Mom suddenly shook with sobs. "Mom!" Rachael squeezed her hand as they leaned into each other. "Mom, it's okay. That's why he was there. It's going to be okay … for all of us. He wants us all to know that he's doing just fine." I covered my face as she added:

"That's when I stopped worrying…

"But, there's something else." Now, eyes drooping and with a silence that kept us wondering, she said, finally: "I have to say this. I'm sorry." She turned to take in each one as she whispered. "I'm just so … sorry. Colt… Daron… Mom… I'm so sorry." More blinking, as the tears flooded.

"Rache—" I said, struggling, "I'm … sorry, too."

Mom gathered her in, and Rachael collapsed into that embrace. The arms that held my sister were the arms that blessed all of us. Mom broke the silence, caressing her hair and asking, "You knew you could come back here?"

As if rising from her dream, Rachael spoke up. "I wasn't really sure except to keep trying, keep pushing and pushing through. Anyhow, I was walking through one of those dark, shadowy, cloudy things. I needed to get to the other side. And I thought I heard something: 'Child.' I thought I heard the word 'Child.'"

"Of course!" said Mrs. Fleury, who had been intensely observing everyone. "You heard me calling you when I said 'Child.' Rachael, you are God's Child! You are coming home to us, little one." There was a moment as we all looked at Mrs. F, with her dangly earrings and bright eyes. "We all wander, and then we find our way home." She reached out for Colt and his two friends. She touched each one on his shoulder or back, and then turned to Sis.

"We never stopped searching, never stopped praying—and you never gave up! I prayed you would listen when I called out for you. You are God's Sweet Child and you know that, don't you?" I was still trying to process this as Mrs. F's light shined on all of us. "He calls us his 'Children of Israel' when he guides us back home."

Mom managed a smile as she said, "I made some soup this morning, would you like some?" Rachael burst out laughing, and there was music in her laugh that carried me back to a time long, long ago. "Mom, you said the magic words! Yes! Can we eat now?"

After we added a few chairs there was enough room for all around the dining table. Mom dished out her beef-and-potato soup and iced tea, and she said a prayer: "Lord Jesus, we thank you for your love, your grace, your forgiveness, and we thank you for Rachael who was lost." I looked up at my mother, tears streaming down her beautiful face.

CHAPTER 20

If God's hand touched me would I know? If so, it would be the same hand that held Rachael. Nearly three weeks gone. Now she was back with us and showing only a little fatigue. This was the same sister I'd grown up with and yet, she was new or different. There were days, not so long ago, when I wanted her gone and would have been pleased to forget her face. That face, that smirk—as if she knew it all but I knew nothing. I watched her now and she looked at me, and there was love. I wanted to love her back, but how?

A chubby baby girl who couldn't sit up. She would roll over and laugh at herself, trying to get upright again. Those plastic donuts that I balanced on her head would make her laugh even more as they tumbled and rolled away from her fat hands. Or, I would wipe tears from her face because her crying seemed to pierce something in me. If I left the room she would be waiting for my return, and ready to smile and play.

Rachael, maybe I can learn to live with you if you just stop breaking my heart.

The police investigation was all tidied up when they finally locked it away in their records cabinet (even if they had no answers). The plans for a community memorial service were tossed and forgotten. The parks crew continued mowing all around the stone bridge and the old playground as if nothing had ever happened in the gently sloping grassland. She had survived for weeks in that Place and emerged on the other side. There was still plenty to discuss but most of the talk was between mother and daughter.

I guess the print shop managed somehow without me, but still I felt I should check in. Just before heading there I glanced over Mom's shoulder again, at an underlined passage in 1st Corinthians. She'd mentioned before about something called the "Epistles" and how they were some of her favorite chapters to study. And—that they were Paul's letters and maybe I could read them, too. So, I jotted on a scrap of paper "chapter 15 v. 16" in case I wanted to look it up later.

John-the-Printer and Marie had smiles and back-slaps for me when I got to the shop. It felt a little like a chapter was closing or that my life might return to normal. Whatever "normal" is, anyway. John started me on a couple of projects such as cleaning out the year's worth of crud from the dreary corner behind the big press. That "small" project turned into an hour of digging out an accumulation of grime, shreds of paper and layer upon layer of lint. John grinned at me when I hauled my filthy self back out. What a mess ... and I loved every moment of it.

Rachael was home.

Sometimes that was true but mostly it felt surreal. This time she might even stick around a while, though, and that put a grin on Colt's face that we hadn't seen since Dad died. Colt was with me the Saturday we rode our bikes to the park, and it just felt right to be back with my brother. First, the "new" park, just to bask in the lush manicured beauty of its trees and walkways with their border flowers. And the little stream trickling down into the pond ... it was almost too sweet and welcoming, but the toddlers sure had a blast exploring all the play equipment. Then, across town we wandered the familiar worn-down paths of the old park with all its self-descriptive graffiti. We pedaled past the neglected tennis courts and netless basketball goals to our most familiar haunt, the stone bridge. There we stood and took it all in. In that little park it didn't take long to recall the misadventures of two brothers and a sister who vanished.

But I was on my own when I cycled the perimeter streets and roads to get a feeling for Rachael's journey. When she wandered home did she find guidance through corn and soybean fields? Or, did she plop down out of the sky on a desolate dirt road? Did she even know we were searching for her? Did she feel abandoned? All worthy questions which would keep nicely until some quiet half-hour when we could sit and get to know each other.

Naturally, I was back atop the old stone bridge when my bike brought me full circle. "God—" I said and cleared my throat. "Um, God, I just want to start by saying thank you. Nothing is possible without you, and I realize that now. I hope you hear me, but I really don't know how to do this. I'm sure you have your reasons for bringing me here, and I don't need to know what they are.

"But, if I could just feel your presence that would be a good thing. And it doesn't have to be now but maybe sometime in the next weeks or months—that would be great. Because I know now that there's someone called the Holy Spirit. And I'm beginning to understand, like my Mom says, that you are Father and that you are also Spirit and you are the Son. That concept is just a little difficult for me. But, if so, it seems like you might be close to me because you are the Son who completely knows everything we've been through. And I thank you, Jesus, for that. For loving us and for showing me what grace means."

How could I not be grateful? If I took a look at my life or if I spent any time at all with these people I loved, I would see that this little world was no longer in my hands. Maybe I was beginning to see the "bigger picture."

At each place around the nearly-abandoned old park I would stop and say thank you. First, I said thanks for my Dad. I moved on. I said thanks for Colt and for my job and for my sweet Mom, who somehow never stopped believing in me. I stopped and said thanks for our grandparents, on both sides. I said thanks for a place to live. I even said thanks for my bike. I moved again and said thanks for a truth that suddenly dawned on me: that God gives us one—and only one—moment to live. So what's the point if we just waste it?

"God," I said as I finally made it back to "my" bridge. "You know Rachael better than I do. Are you with her right now? Because if you are I hope you will protect her. She needs you. I need her, too, but I don't know how to let her know so maybe you could do that for me. Thank you. For Rachael." I hopped back on the bike, and we headed home. If God heard my prayer would I know?

CHAPTER 21

"For if the dead are not raised, then Christ has not been raised either. And if Christ has not been raised, your faith is futile; you are still in your sins. Then those also who have fallen asleep in Christ are lost. If only for this life we have hope in Christ, we are of all people most to be pitied.

"But Christ has indeed been raised from the dead, the firstfruits of those who have fallen asleep. For since death came through a man, the resurrection of the dead comes also through a man. For as in Adam all die, so in Christ all will be made alive…"*

* (1st Corinthians 15:16-22)

I read Paul's words at my place, from 1st Corinthians, in Chapter 15 and starting at Verse 16. I read some more from this Epistle, but those verses kind of stayed with me that night and on into the next day. It struck me that Adam was connected to Christ, through our "old friends" Abraham and Sarah. One wouldn't have happened without the other. It made it kind of a neat little package. Most things in the Bible were a bit of a struggle, but this picture was less fuzzy.

The other part of Paul's writing was about sin. Why did he have to bring that up? I suppose it was something for me to deal with like all the other messy stuff I had going on those days. Well, someday…

Later, we sat there with Mom on her couch (which she called her "napping" couch) and enjoyed some crackers and cheese. Just the four of us. It might have been any other ordinary day, when Mom was about ready to go to work, and Colt was annoying me by flipping his hair around in my face. So I bonked him. I noticed Mom was holding Rachael's hand. They were chatting about something … I believe it had to do with a new pair of slippers.

In Memory:
Patrice Irene Woner
1951-2000

...For I received from the Lord what I also passed on to you: The Lord Jesus, on the night he was betrayed, took bread, and when he had given thanks, he broke it and said, "This is my body, which is for you; do this in remembrance of me..." *(1 Corinthians 11:23-24)*

facebook.com/
The GrandDad Tree